# Samuel shrugged out of his suit jacket and laid it across the chaise lounge.

He gripped the knot of his tie, loosening it with small deliberate strokes that inexplicably kindled heat between Arlie's thighs. Finally, he slid the tie from his neck, casting it off across his discarded jacket.

"Better?" he asked.

Arlie padded barefoot across the space between them.

"Almost." Lifting her hands to his neck, she undid the button closest to his collar. Then another. And another.

Dizzy with desire, Arlie tilted her face up to his. The air was alive with electricity, crackling and sizzling with anticipation.

"All my life, I could have anything I wanted." Cupping her jaw, he ran the pad of his thumb over her lower lip. "Except you."

Arlie's breath came in irregular bursts, something deep inside her tightening at his admission. "You want me?"

Samuel only looked at her, silent but saying all.

*Yes.*

\* \* \*

*Corner Office Confessions* by Cynthia St. Aubin is part of The Kane Heirs series.

Dear Reader,

As a confirmed candy addict, there was something I loved about the idea of a family-owned confectionary company becoming a billion-dollar empire, eventually to be inherited by three siblings named after famous detectives by their mystery-loving mother.

Also a sucker for a quiet, serious, somewhat misanthropic hero, I couldn't help but sympathize with Samuel Kane, once a painfully shy bookworm and now the CEO of Kane Foods, who hatches a plot to rid himself—and the company—of his wastrel playboy twin brother, Mason, by tempting him to break their father's "no company romances" rule. Enter talented food stylist and hot mess Arlie Banks— the woman Mason had chased since prep school but never caught.

Concealing secrets of her own—a long-standing crush on Samuel being one of them—Arlie proves not to be the pliant pawn Samuel had anticipated, and before long, he finds himself in danger of being caught in his own trap.

I sincerely hope you enjoy *Corner Office Confessions*, book one in The Kane Heirs series, and I would love it if you come find me on Facebook to say hello!

Sweet reading!

*Cynthia*

# CYNTHIA ST. AUBIN

---

## CORNER OFFICE CONFESSIONS

Sincere gratitude to my talented editor, Charles Griemsman, and my amazing agent lady, Christine Witthohn, without whose careful and patient encouragement and suggestions the Kane Heirs wouldn't exist.

My eternal thanks to my Emotional Support Human and critique partner, Kerrigan Byrne, for talking me from literary ledges, and plot-genie Sara Lunsford for making Samuel's story considerably less lumpy.

A special thank-you to Angela Yeung, food stylist extraordinaire, for acquainting me with all the tricks of the trade. I'll never look at gravy the same way again.

Finally, thank you to the readers, who make it possible for me to do what I love. You're my favorite.

# HARLEQUIN®
# DESIRE™

Recycling programs for this product may not exist in your area.

ISBN-13: 978-1-335-73569-0

Corner Office Confessions

Copyright © 2022 by Cynthia St. Aubin

For questions and comments about the quality of this book, please contact us at CustomerService@Harlequin.com.

Harlequin Enterprises ULC
22 Adelaide St. West, 41st Floor
Toronto, Ontario M5H 4E3, Canada
www.Harlequin.com

Printed in U.S.A.

**Cynthia St. Aubin** wrote her first play at age eight and made her brothers perform it for the admission price of gum wrappers. When she was tall enough to reach the top drawer of her parents' dresser, she began pilfering her mother's secret stash of romance novels and has been in love with love ever since. A confirmed cheese addict, she lives in Texas with a handsome musician.

### Books by Cynthia St. Aubin

**The Kane Heirs**

*Corner Office Confessions*

Visit the Author Profile page at Harlequin.com, or www.cynthiastaubin.com, for more titles.

You can also find Cynthia St. Aubin on Facebook, along with other Harlequin Desire authors, at Facebook.com/harlequindesireauthors!

To everyone who's ever had to start over.

And to my husband, who showed me
it's never too late to find happily-ever-after.

# One

Now was not the time to think about the kiss.

It had happened ten years ago, but Arlington Banks could still taste him. The roasted grain sweetness of beer snuck at a high school keg party. His adrenaline, sharp and metallic on her tongue. She could still feel the ghost of his fingers trailing up her ribs, goose bumps spilling from her scalp to her shoes.

Now, after a decade, they were in the same building.

Arlie stole one last glance at her reflection in the brushed metal elevator doors and tucked an escaped tendril back into the chignon she'd spent hours trying to make look effortless.

Tilting her chin to one side and then the other, she managed to confirm her carefully applied makeup was in place despite the door seam dividing her reflection.

And divided was exactly how she felt. Half of her

knew that agreeing to a job interview with Samuel Kane, CEO of Kane Foods International, was perhaps the worst idea she'd ever had. The other half knew it was the best option given her circumstances.

*Circumstances.*

A rather polite word for the soul-sucking chaos she had recently dragged herself through.

Nails digging half-moons into her palms, she watched the glowing green numbers flash on the panel to the right of the doors: 12…13…14… Ten more to go before she reached the exalted floor that served as the executive offices.

The elevator car eased to a stop with a musical ping. Arlie took a deep breath, hoping the small, cold ball of her stomach would lower back to its normal position.

No such luck.

Stepping out onto the twenty-fourth floor, she turned and came face-to-face with French doors roughly a story tall.

This was the place, all right. The Kanes had never been much for understatement. At least, not in the fifteen years she had known the family.

A mechanical buzz sounded as she approached and the doors swung smoothly inward. Arlie bit back an unintentional gasp.

Acres of travertine marble flooring stretched before her, the sweeping curve of a grand staircase flanked on either side by intricately carved wrought-iron railing. The chandelier dangling above it was a hurricane of crystal shards forever suspended in a violent vortex. At its apex, a soaring opera house ceiling had been intricately painted a tranquil blue interrupted only by puffy clouds and cavorting cherubs. Around the border, expertly painted architectural details gave the impression of hand-carved stonework.

She had learned about this kind of hyper realistic paintings in an art history survey course in college once upon a time.

*Trompe l'oeil*. To deceive the eye.

In her experience, eyes weren't the only things the Kane family was capable of deceiving.

Arlie wasn't sure how long she had been standing there, mouth agape, when a smooth, honeyed voice dropped her back into the present.

"You must be Miss Banks."

Tearing her gaze away from the ceiling, Arlie noticed the reception desk tucked neatly against the wall. Behind the lacquered expanse of inlaid wood, a petite brunette with designer eyeglasses beamed a warm wide smile at her. A small plaque at the desk's beveled edge proclaimed her to be Evelyn Norris, Receptionist.

"I am. I have—"

"A nine o'clock interview with Mr. Kane," Evelyn Norris, Receptionist finished for her with practiced efficiency. "Yes, Miss Westbrook informed me."

"*Samuel* Kane," Arlie said. Lord help her if she ended up at the desk of the wrong Kane. Not that there was a right Kane, if history was any indication.

"Yes, I see that." Evelyn's eyes flicked toward the oversized monitor on the desk. "If you wouldn't mind taking a seat, I'll let him know you're here."

"Of course." Arlie readjusted the strap of her laptop bag. Within the lobby's cavernous height, the echo of her stiletto heels sounded like gunshots as she wandered over to the waiting area.

Like her shoes, the rest of her outfit had been selected with almost surgical precision. A tight—but not too tight—fitting pencil skirt. A tailored—but not too tailored—crisp white V-necked blouse that revealed the barest hint of cleavage. The hairstyle had been the one element she'd agonized over. Standing in front of the mirror cursing her thick, wheat-colored strands, she'd summarily vetoed long and loose as too casual and nixed half pulled back as too indecisive before deciding on the simple updo.

Settling onto the buttery leather, Arlie drew her phone out of her bag and scrolled through her email to the message that had tossed her world straight off its axis.

Good afternoon,

I am reaching out on behalf of Mr. Samuel Kane, who wished for me to acquaint you with an immediate opening for Senior Food Stylist at Kane Foods International. Starting salary for the position would be $85k annually with full benefits. Should you be interested in learning more about this opportunity, please reach out at your earliest convenience.

Best,

Charlotte Westbrook

Executive Assistant to Mr. Parker Kane

Mr. Parker Kane. Arlie had nearly deleted the message when she'd seen that name. She remembered the Kane family patriarch in exceedingly alarming detail. His cold, steely gaze. His thin, perpetually unsmiling mouth. The intricate ways he'd found to keep her aware that, as the daughter of the Kane family's personal chef, she had been inferior by association.

But Mr. *Samuel* Kane. That was a whole other matter. Eldest of the three Kane siblings by a mere hour, Samuel was a book nerd turned multimillionaire CEO. That name, along with the *should you be interested* had ultimately caught her interest. Arlie had read that phrase approximately seventy-eight times.

It wasn't the opportunity she was interested in, per se, though the position aligned alarmingly well with her qualifications.

She was interested in not having to choose which bill she would pay late each month. She was interested in no longer working high-end service for tables of wealthy businessmen who somehow managed to ogle and insult her at the same time. She was interested in piecing back together the rubble of her life after the complete and total disaster that the last six months had been.

"It appears Mr. Kane is running just a few minutes late," Evelyn informed her. "He asked me to convey his sincere apologies."

As if any Kane was capable of sincerity.

Her brief encounters with Mason Kane, Samuel's twin brother, had certainly taught her that. Pompous, popular, and persistent, Mason had dogged her heels from the second she'd crossed the threshold of the private school they had all attended. Achievement had been tantamount among Lennox Finch Academy's coveted virtues. Some people broke records in high school track. Some students got their names on the honor roll.

Arlie's lone distinction within those hallowed halls? She'd been the only female to resist Mason Kane's self-professed ample charms. Four long years of his asking her out in increasingly dramatic and creative ways only to be rebuffed each and every time. All the while,

Arlie's attention had been fixed on shy, serious Samuel, on whom she'd had an ardent, desperate crush.

"No trouble at all," Arlie assured her. Reaching into her bag, she drew out her leather portfolio. A small swell of pride loosened anxiety's grip on her chest as she paged through the glossy photographs from cookbooks, magazines and digital ads. Glasses of iced tea with their thirst-inducing beads of condensation. Perfectly medium-rare steaks, pink juices anointing pristine white plates. Vibrantly green roasted broccolini, coarse sea salt scattered like honeymoon rose petals over the crisped crowns.

She had been good at this, once upon a time. A rare double threat who both styled the food *and* took the photographs. The thought was a soothing balm to the open, aching wound that losing her dream job had ripped open.

Made all the deeper by the fact that she'd brought it on herself.

"Mr. Kane is ready for you." Evelyn marched around the front of her desk, a gentle incline of her head indicating Arlie was meant to follow her.

Together, they bustled down the hallway to yet another elevator. Evelyn flashed her badge at a small black panel before pressing the single button.

The only way was up.

"Here we are." Evelyn held the elevator door when they arrived at their destination, allowing Arlie to exit first.

The fabled twenty-fifth floor didn't look like an office so much as a penthouse apartment. Wood parquet floors. Intricately woven Persian rugs. Rooms with curio cabinets full of objets d' art and ankle-deep carpeting.

Directly across from the elevator, a wall-sized mirror in gilded frame hovered behind a table displaying an army of pictures. Arlie floated over to them, overcome by a wave of nostalgia that almost toppled her off her carefully chosen shoes.

Kanes jumping horses. Kanes posing with purebred dogs. Kanes holding aloft the limp carcasses of sleek feathered ducks and geese.

All three Kane siblings lined up before the gigantic stone-lion-flanked fireplace of Fair Weather Hall. Only child that she was, Arlie had always been fascinated by the idea of siblings. Looking at the picture now, she felt a similar pang of longing. She had remembered the late Mrs. Kane explaining to her that she'd chosen their names based on her much-beloved detective novels—Marlowe, her only daughter, and the twins: Mason and Samuel.

And there he was. The Samuel Kane she had met for the first time when they were both thirteen years old. A green-eyed, dark-haired, sullen boy with wire-rimmed glasses, always standing a good foot away from his twin brother and his sister. Arlie would have bet her Nikon D6 that the hand mysteriously missing from Samuel's left side hid a book behind his back.

"Miss Banks?" Evelyn had made it halfway down the hall before realizing she'd lost Arlie.

"So sorry," Arlie said, trotting to catch up.

"Mr. Kane's office," Evelyn announced before knocking exactly three times on a large wooden door.

"Come," the muffled voice ordered from the other side, a strange mix of irritation and command.

Arlie's stomach performed an impromptu death roll as Evelyn gingerly turned the ornate handle and peeked into the opening. "Miss Banks for you."

"Fine."

Evelyn Norris stepped back, giving Arlie's elbow an encouraging squeeze before shuffling off down the hall.

Heart rattling against her ribs like a trapped bird, Arlie squared her shoulders, tilted her chin up, and opened the door.

Her first thought when she saw Samuel Kane standing beside a desk roughly the size of a boxcar was that she shouldn't have brought her portfolio, she should have brought a crash helmet. Because the second her eyes locked with his, her knees decided to turn to butter.

A thousand times she had rehearsed this scene in her head. A thousand times she had failed to adequately prepare herself for the man standing before her.

The Samuel Kane she had invented for these mental practice runs was a slightly older version of the quiet, studious teenager she had known. Tall and lean, maybe with a good start on a receding hairline. Definitely wearing some kind of pretentiously recognizable designer suit.

The suit part she'd been right about.

Damned if she hadn't been dead wrong about how that suit would fit him.

His coat hung from a polished mahogany coat rack to the left of his desk, allowing Arlie an unfettered view of the pale blue shirt clinging to his broad, rounded shoulders and a torso clearly honed by hours, days, probably years, in the gym. A crisp sapphire tie hung down the center of his chest, anchored in place by a gleaming gilded lion tiepin. Below the tawny leather belt circling a lean waist, the fitted pinstripe slacks hugged the powerful, corded muscles of his long legs.

Then there was his face.

Many an afternoon when she had come to Fair Weather to help her mother with the food for a large gathering, she'd invented elaborate excuses to steal glimpses of Samuel while he'd sequestered himself in the family's library, a pile of books next to him on the Regency end table. From her covert vantage, she'd watched as he'd turned page after page, pausing only to push his glasses up his nose with the tip of his left index finger at regular intervals.

As a young man, he'd had an almost poetic sensibility with full sensitive lips and prominent cheekbones, a lock of dark hair flopping over his brow. The hair and lips remained intact, but years and a goodly dose of testosterone had broadened his jaw, chiseling it into a dangerous outcropping above the crisp angle of his starched collar. Beyond the actual changes in his features, Samuel looked like every ounce of his relentless thirst for knowledge had been distilled into hunger itself. Lean. Predatory. Ruthless.

"Arlie Banks," Samuel said, coming around his desk. "Thank you for coming."

She hadn't realized she'd frozen in the entryway until he closed the distance between them with purposeful strides. When he was close enough for Arlie to catch a current of soap, aftershave and pressed wool, he held out his hand.

After a beat of hesitation, she slid her small, sweaty palm into his, surprised by the electric jolt that shot straight to her heart when his fingers closed over hers.

"Of course," she said, trying to seem confident and

calm as she met the eerie golden-green eyes he'd inherited from his late mother. "Thank you for thinking of me."

"I didn't." He motioned her toward the chair directly opposite from his expansive desk.

"Oh?" Arlie tried to ignore the stab of disappointment as she primly seated herself.

"It was Marlowe." Samuel walked around behind his desk and slid into the wide wing-backed leather chair with practiced ease.

"Oh," was the most intelligent answer Arlie could manage.

Marlowe Kane, one grade below and several levels of social sophistication above Arlie, had mostly ignored her during high school. Sometime after college, Arlie had been surprised to receive a connection request from her on a social media employment site. No one had been more shocked than Arlie when she discovered that Marlowe had traded in her pom-poms for an MBA and a job as the corporate comptroller at Kane Foods International.

"She mentioned that you were the artistic director of *Gastronomie*, but that you'd recently left the company."

A single bead of cold sweat crawled down Arlie's ribs like an unwelcome insect as she silently prayed that he didn't ask for any further details. "That's correct."

Samuel leaned forward in his chair, light from the floor-to-ceiling windows behind him gilding the crown of his dark, sleek head. "Why?"

# Two

Samuel Kane had made millions of dollars for Kane Foods International by reading people. A twitch of the eyebrow, a twist of the lips, a nervous glance to the side—all signs of weakness. Weakness could be useful.

At this precise moment, Arlie Banks's features betrayed an internal battle of exponential magnitude. True, he was having a harder time than he had anticipated in gauging her reactions. Not, he told himself, because her wide sky-blue eyes made thoughts of business hard to hold in his head. And certainly not because he was overcome by the inexplicable urge to extract whatever pin held her smooth blond coiffure in place to see if her hair still spilled down her back as it had when they were seventeen.

*Definitely not* either of those things.

"Why did I leave *Gastronomie*?" she repeated. A clear bid to buy herself time.

"That's what I asked."

Her eyes widened a fraction, the edges of her teeth sinking into her lower lip in a way that made Samuel's pants feel as if they'd been tailored too severely in the crotch.

*Fear.*

He could practically smell it through her perfume, which was an oddly intoxicating mix of wildflowers, rain and silk.

"The chief marketing officer and I had insurmountable artistic differences." She shifted in her chair, tugging the hem of her skirt toward her knees.

*Lie.*

A more scrupulous man might have felt a pang of guilt. He'd asked her an unfair question, and he knew it. Not because the question wasn't relevant to the interview. Because the answer didn't matter.

Arlie Banks already had the job.

The second she had stepped into his office, Samuel had known she would be perfect.

Not as their senior food stylist, though his research confirmed she was amply capable.

For lead ingénue in a personal project Samuel had conceived to oust his womanizing wastrel of a twin brother, Mason, from Kane Foods International.

His reason for doing so was as simple as it was crucial: to clear his path to the head of a company he'd done his best to build and Mason his best to destroy. This morning had only helped solidify his resolve. Mason had, in his usual fashion, failed to show up for the interview they were supposed to conduct together.

For a full twenty minutes, Samuel had kept Arlie waiting in the lobby while he sat in his office, seething. What had begun as mild irritation bred into a boiling black rage as the antique grandfather clock in the corner expensively announced the passage of time with small, metallic clicks.

All his life, or for as much of it as he could remember, Samuel had been waiting on his twin.

It had begun the day they were born, when Samuel spent his first hour of life cooling his recently inked heels in the nursery while their eager parents and a small army of nurses coaxed Mason to make his leisurely arrival. When high school rolled around, Samuel sat in the driver's seat of their shared car while Mason squeezed, hugged, kissed and winked his way through the legion of his female admirers.

Just last week, it had come to a maddening head when Mason not only showed up half an hour late to a meeting with an important investor Samuel had courted for two years, but also managed to receive full credit for brokering the deal. A victory their father, Parker Kane, had profusely congratulated Mason for. As he had in so many instances before.

Some things never changed.

Arlie Banks certainly had.

The girl he remembered had darted around Fair Weather Hall with a kind of effortless charm. Tomboyish and sprightly. Carefree and unpretentious. Completely oblivious of his twin brother pathetically panting in her wake.

True, Samuel had harbored his own brief and exceedingly mild infatuation with her.

But then, during most of the years of their acquaintance, Samuel had been little more than a walking hormone.

The woman seated across from Samuel could just about reduce any grown man to that state. Though her waist was every bit as slim as it had been when she'd sat in front of him in sophomore Shakespearian English, dangerous curves now filled out her tailored skirt and blouse.

Mason Kane was a dead man.

One look at Arlie, and Mason was sure to break their father's only hard-and-fast corporate rule: No. Company. Romances.

"I can certainly see where creative difference could be an issue," Samuel said, fully aware he'd hesitated a beat too long in his reply. "That shouldn't be a problem here as I believe you already know our chief marketing officer. My brother, Mason Kane."

"Is that so?" Surprise shaved a metric ton of worry from Arlie's face, briefly revealing the ghost of the girl he had known.

"It is," Samuel said. "In fact, he was supposed to join us for—"

"Well, if it isn't Arlie Banks."

Samuel glanced up sharply as Mason swept into his office trailing expensive aftershave and lame apologies in his wake.

"Don't shoot." Mason slung his Louis Vuitton briefcase down on the table and raised his hands in supplication. "I got stuck in traffic."

*Right*, Samuel thought. If *traffic* was code for *leggy blonde several years his junior.*

"So glad you could grace us with your presence," Samuel quipped, not bothering to rise from his chair.

With the entitlement of a man who took what he wanted without asking, Mason reached over to a chair at the four-top table and swung it closer to Arlie's than Samuel would have liked. Shucking off his suit jacket, he tossed it haphazardly over the edge of the desk. "What'd I miss?"

Perhaps because Arlie had known them both since they were teenagers, Samuel wondered how they looked to her side by side now. They were identical twins, but in reality, the habits acquired in their thirty years on the planet had begun to sand away some of the similarities they had once shared.

Where Samuel's chiseled physique was a testament to the precisely calibrated gym routine he pushed through for exactly sixty minutes every morning, Mason had the casual musculature of an avid pool party attendee and the glowing tan to match. The sun had also been at work on his brother's hair, gilding casual waves always in need of a trim.

Arlie seemed to appreciate the effect, given how she furtively moistened her lips with the pointed pink tip of her tongue and recrossed her legs in Mason's direction.

Samuel bit down on his irritation. This was, after all, exactly what he'd wanted.

Wasn't it?

"How long has it been?" Mason asked, running a hand through his wind-tousled hair as he turned toward Arlie.

"Twelve years," she answered, picking at an invisible thread on her skirt. "Give or take."

Twelve years, five months, ten days. Not that Samuel had been counting. It just so happened that the last time they'd seen Arlie Banks was the night of their high school graduation, an occasion that loomed prominently in his memory.

It was the one and only time in his life that Samuel Kane had leveraged his identical twin status to pretend to be his brother.

For reasons he dare not think of while Arlie Banks sat across the desk from him.

"How is it that you don't look a day over twenty?" Mason leaned forward, pretending to scrutinize Arlie's features.

Samuel suppressed an eye roll. There was no math to calculate exactly how many times he'd seen his brother employ this particular line in restaurants, bars, executive receptions, the coat check line at Vetri Cucina.

"As charming as this stroll down memory lane is," Samuel said, "perhaps we ought to ask Miss Banks questions that actually pertain to her qualifications?"

"*Miss* Banks?" Mason mimicked. "Awfully formal for someone who's seen you naked."

A less cerebral, self-possessed man might have leapt the desk to throttle his brother with his own Armani necktie. Samuel could have lived another thirty years without remembering that particular humiliation belonging to the evening of their sixteenth birthday.

Clearly, Arlie's memories of that night were just as vivid, if the rabid roses blooming in her cheeks were any indication.

"Oh, lighten up, Sam-*Mule*," Mason said, employing the much-loathed nickname he'd saddled Samuel with after a regrettable debate team trip during their freshman year. "We're just catching up."

Pressing the tip of his index finger to the corner of his twitching eye, Samuel cleared his throat and sat up straighter in his chair. "In any case, Kane Foods International has decided to branch out into the health and wellness industry and, as a part of that effort, we'll need to employ a significantly different marketing angle than we've heretofore—"

"What my clearly anal retentive brother is attempting to say is that we need someone to make it look like we haven't been mostly peddling liver-fattening confectionary since the mid 1800s."

"Kane Foods has been responsible for supplying families with quality goods since 1834," Samuel began.

"With only five American dollars in his pocket and a hand-built cart—" Mason continued, his tone mocking "—Damien Hetherington O'Kane began the business that now clears twenty-six billion in profit annually. Next thing we know, you'll be whipping out that black-and-white photo of the saltwater taffy lines." Mason paused to roll his eyes. "Jesus, you sound like Dad."

This rankled Samuel more than anything else his brother had said.

Parker Kane, patriarch and Chairman Emeritus of Kane Foods International, the man whom Samuel had idolized—and Mason had alternately disobeyed and ignored since their joint arrival on the planet—favored his second son to the point of embarrassment.

Samuel's mostly. But occasionally the board of directors and the executive team, who both endured his effusive apologies and excuses for Mason's tardiness and frequent absence.

"I have experience with directional shifts in branding." For the third time since she'd entered his office, Arlie reached up and tucked a straying pale gold tendril back behind the delicate shell of her ear. The perfect metaphor for the wildness Samuel knew lurked just below her calm surface.

"I'd love to hear more about that." Mason propped an elbow on his knee and rested his chin on his fist.

If Samuel hadn't known better, he might suspect that his brother was actually listening.

"At Stride Global, we started as a manufacturer of vitamin packets but transitioned to energy shots and hangover gel packs."

"That's quite a conversion," Mason said before Samuel had the chance.

There had been a period, however brief, that they might have spoken this sentence in unison. These kinds of twin phenomena had evaporated around the time they'd achieved puberty. Right along with his fiercely protective older-twin instinct.

"It was," she said. "I have to admit that styling is a pretty significant challenge when it comes to little foil packets, but retaining our emphasis on non-GMO ingredients helped."

Mason nodded, pretending to look thoughtful.

Samuel rose from his chair, pacing around the moat of his desk. "Let me ask you this."

Arlie Banks flinched.

*Interesting.*

"Supply Side West is coming up. The biggest health and wellness supplier event of the year."

"I've heard of it." Arlie's eyes met his and darted away just as quickly.

*Very* interesting.

"We have a number of important partners coming and could use a solid presence there. Particularly in regard to our booth concept. Is that something you would feel comfortable assisting with?"

"Absolutely," she answered far too quickly.

"Of course, it's not all work" Mason said. "I have it on good authority that we'll be hosting several client appreciation events which would benefit from your attendance."

"From an artistic angle?" Arlie asked, glancing at Mason below her fringe of dark lashes.

"Let's call it an energetic angle." Mason's broad smile displayed one of the ten thousand reasons they were no longer identical. A small, faint scar at the corner of his mouth that silvered when stretched.

"I would be happy to supply both." Arlie's grin matched Mason's in brightness.

Samuel bit the inside of his cheek hard enough to taste copper. "Arlie Banks," he said, hating the pomposity of his own voice at that precise moment, "we would be delighted to offer you the position of senior food stylist."

The wry expression on his twin's face suggested he might already be contemplating several other positions he might like to offer her.

*Good.* Good, but irritating to the point of madness.

Arlie stood and held out her hand. "I accept."

Mason beat him to the punch, clasping Arlie's hand and pumping it up and down enthusiastically. "Glad to have you aboard."

Samuel settled for a curt nod of approval.

He did this because he could summon the feel of her skin on his whenever he wished.

Because the night of their high school graduation, he had pretended to be his brother when he'd kissed Arlie Banks.

# Three

The oversized, polished wood door swung wide, the beep of a security system announcing Arlie's arrival at Retrospect, the upscale vintage store in Philadelphia's trendy Fishtown neighborhood. More art gallery than thrift store, the shop was clean, white-walled and spacious. All the better to show off the dresses artfully arranged like installations at strategic points in the interior.

"Be right with you." A warm, throaty voice floated out to her from somewhere in the back.

"Damn right you will," Arlie called back with far more bravado than she felt.

The simple black curtain behind the counter parted abruptly, revealing the store's owner.

One look at her, and it was easy to see why Philadelphia's moneyed elite lined up to shove their cash into her pockets. With wide eyes the exact color of burnt sugar, full lips painted a stylish matte burgundy, gleaming onyx hair knotted into braids at her temples and tumbling into riotous natural curls, Kassidy Nichols was a show stopper. An effect only amplified by the simple but elegantly cut white frock that hugged her curves and made her skin glow a rich sepia brown.

"You know," Kassidy said, tapping her chin, "you look just like my former best friend. Arlington Banks? But I know you can't *be* Arlington Banks, because she hasn't returned my numerous calls."

Truth be told, Arlie hadn't exactly been looking forward to this interaction for this very reason. She could practically *feel* the relentless engine of her brilliant best friend's brain working.

The valedictorian of their class at Lennox Finch Academy, Kassidy had bonded with Arlie over a shared dislike of *The Great Gatsby* in freshman AP English. Ironic, considering the herd of wealthy thoroughbred classmates that they—two girls from suburban middle class families—found themselves trotting awkwardly among.

Always the rebel to Arlie's compulsive rule-following nerd, Kassidy had graduated from Harvard Law School and completed one year with the most prestigious firm in Philadelphia before scandalizing her family by announcing that her considerable mental gifts were best used helping lonely vintage gowns find good homes. Within her first year of business, Kassidy had paid back the initial loan she'd borrowed to get Retrospect off the ground. By her second, she'd earned enough to purchase her stylish condo in Rittenhouse Square outright.

"I'm so sorry." Arlie shifted on her painfully pinching heels. "I've just had a lot going on lately and—"

*"You're sorry?"* Kassidy mimicked. "No, *I'm* sorry. We take American Express, cash, checks and, occasionally, wire transfers from Swiss bank accounts, but I'm afraid lame-ass excuses aren't accepted here."

"Your Honor," Arlie said, clasping her hands in supplication, "I plead guilty to violating the communication requirements of the best friend contract and cast myself on the mercy of the court."

The subtle softening of her friend's features sent a gust of relief through Arlie's tight chest.

"Since this is your first offense, the court will commute your sentence to two dinners and a *Bridgerton* marathon. *If,*" Kassidy added, pointing an accusatory finger at Arlie, "you bring the wine."

"I do so swear." Arlie placed one hand on the counter and lifted the other, open palm facing her friend.

"Now." Kassidy scanned her from foot to head, missing nothing. "Are you going to tell me why you look like you're auditioning for a role as one of Christian Gray's secretaries?"

*Well, shit.*

Arlie took a breath and readied herself to deliver the answer she had rehearsed on the way over.

"As it happens, I had a job interview." Knowing that Kassidy read her as easily as an illustrated storybook, Arlie tried—unsuccessfully—to evict all thoughts of Samuel Kane from her head. As if in protest, her mind offered up a contact sheet of her favorite visual snapshots of the time they'd spent together. The expensive fabric of his shirt worshipping the muscular shoulders beneath. The way he cut through the space of his office like a shark.

And God, his eyes. The intensity of his gaze.

He'd known she was lying. Of that much, Arlie was sure. She just hoped he hadn't guessed the full extent of her lie.

"Spill it, Banks," Kassidy said, snapping her back to reality. "Immediately if not sooner."

"It's just a temporary corporate gig," Arlie said, trying to sound breezy and vague. "Just some part-time consulting work. But they made an offer."

Kassidy's sculptural curls caught the light as she shook her head ruefully. "Lady, have I taught you nothing?"

"What?" Arlie asked, hoping to buy herself time to think.

Kassidy crossed her arms over her chest. "You are, without question, the worst liar I've ever met."

Shoulders sagging, Arlie exhaled the breath it felt like she'd been holding since her visit to Samuel's office earlier that morning. "Meet the new senior food stylist for Kane Foods International."

"Kane Foods International," Kassidy repeated as if the ruthlessly bright motor of her brain had become bogged down with swamp weeds. "*Kane* Foods International?"

Arlie nodded, knowing when *not* to talk being one of the things she'd learned under her best friend's tutelage.

"Well, now I know what that disastrous chignon is about. You must be covering the scar from your lobotomy." Her friend's eyes flashed as a deep rose-red bloomed beneath her smooth cheeks, warming them to a russet hue.

"I know," Arlie said, collapsing over the counter with her chin in her hands.

"These are the *Kanes*. The *buy you, sell you, crush your small business, eat your soul and destroy your family to expand our boathouse* Kanes. The ones we said were everything that was wrong with wealth distribution. The ones we swore we would never end up like."

"I know," Arlie repeated. She felt her throat begin to constrict, unwelcome emotion threatening to hijack her thin veneer of calm.

"*Do* you?" Kassidy's normally rich contralto rose to a rusty-edged soprano. "After what happened with your mother and Daddy Kane—"

"Can we fucking *not*?" Arlie snapped, surprised by the sudden solar flare of anger. From the moment Samuel's email had arrived in her in-box, she'd been choking out the overwhelming urge to scream at the mere sight of the name Kane. Of what that name had done to her father. To her family.

"Easy, Banks." Kassidy's soft, warm hand covered Arlie's on the glossy counter.

Instantly regretful, Arlie dialed down her emotional thermostat and exhaled a long, slow breath. "I'm sorry," she said. "I just can't think about that right now. Not with everything else going on."

"Look, I know that things have been rough since you resigned *Gastronomie*."

Since she'd *resigned Gastronomie*.

Guilt added to the rapidly growing tar pool of self-loathing spreading in her middle.

She may have become an accomplished liar of late, but this was the first deliberate falsehood she'd ever told her best friend.

"If it's the money—" Kassidy began.

"No," Arlie interrupted, all too aware of the tears welling in her eyes. She thought of sprinting out of the shop before Kassidy could ask the inevitable question that would open the floodgates once and for all.

"Hey," her best friend said, the constant undercurrent of lightly mocking humor giving way to genuine concern. "You okay?"

And with that, every ounce of pain, worry, fear and desperation came flying directly out of Arlie's already stinging tear ducts. It wasn't just crying, but back-breaking, hiccoughing, body-wrenching sobs.

On cue, Kassidy came around from behind the desk and wrapped Arlie in the first fiercely protective hug she'd experienced since her mother's death five years ago. She'd lost her father to cancer only last year, but their bond had always been tenuous at best. The realization only made her sob harder.

"Shhhh," Kassidy soothed, her hand making slow circles between Arlie's shoulder blades. "It's all right. Everything is going to be all right."

Arlie could no longer remember a time when she believed those words. She simply stood there, letting herself be held, careful to keep her wet cheek away from the pristine fabric of her best friend's dress.

"Anyway," Kassidy said, "I know what this is all *really* about."

Without warning, Arlie's stomach took a roller coaster death drop toward her shoes. "You do?"

"Of course I do. You're just trying to find a way to realize your misguided adolescent fantasy of jumping young Samuel Kane's bones."

"I am *not*." Arlie pulled away, color flooding her

cheeks because, ever since setting her eyes on him this morning, she'd been feverishly fanaticizing about that very thing. A flickering reel of lurid scenarios, interrupted only by intermittent panic attacks.

Her personal favorite had involved Samuel raking the items off his fastidiously organized desk to bend her over it. Even now, she could still feel his breath hot on her neck. The smooth, cool polished wood hard against her cheek. Hands that held so many books dragging her skirt roughly over her hips, pausing only to push her panties to the side before filling her with his hot, hard—

"Jesus." Kassidy's mouth twisted into a smirk as the dimple Arlie had always coveted appeared at the corner of her lips. "You're doing it right now."

"That's totally unfair," Arlie protested. "That's like saying don't think about a pink elephant."

"Or Samuel Kane's studious cock."

Arlie snorted despite herself, some measure of the grief evaporating from her aching heart. "Point is, there was nothing between Samuel and me when we were teenagers and there's nothing between us now."

"Please." Kassidy released Arlie, walking toward Retrospect's entrance to busy herself fussing with the dramatic floral arrangement on the round table opposite the entryway. "I've never witnessed two humans trying so hard to *not* look like they like each other."

A heady surge of unexpected pleasure heated Arlie's ears. "Whatever," she said, employing a term they'd passed back and forth in high school as often as sticks of gum and coded notes.

"I'm serious." Kassidy plucked out the long green stem of a peony and relocated it two inches to the left.

"It was pathetic. You side-eye humping him every time his nose was buried in a book."

"There may be some merit to that assessment," Arlie admitted. "But he didn't even know I existed."

Kassidy said nothing, but something in the way her posture stiffened made Arlie's antennae twitch.

"Or did he?" Arlie joined her friend at the table, a cold ball gathering in the center of her chest. Though she was no match for her best friend in terms of raw mental prowess, she'd spent a decade studying her like meteorologists studied weather maps, and for the same reasons. Her immediate future had often been determined by a mischievous smirk, a stormy gaze. "What aren't you telling me?"

Kassidy's usually regal posture deflated. "This information is not going to help you."

"I'll be the judge of that." Now it was Arlie's turn to cross her arms over her chest.

The corners of Kassidy's mouth tugged downward, her eyes soft and shining. "He...wanted to ask you to prom."

Arlie's face stung as if she'd been slapped.

Time seemed to slow as she looked at her friend. "How do you know?" Arlie demanded.

"Because he tracked me down after advanced trig one day and asked me how likely you'd be to say yes."

"And what did you tell him?"

Kassidy pressed her lips together and drew in a breath. "I told him that...it wasn't my place to speak for you."

"But it was your place to speak *to* me," Arlie said, shaking her head. "Why didn't you tell me?"

"Because I'd either have ruined the surprise if he did

ask or get you all amped up just to be let down if he didn't. Frankly, I was as excited about either of those options as I was the idea of you being involved with a Kane." Kassidy fixed her with a meaningful look.

Sure enough, Arlie was now feeling an odd mix of those things. Excitement that he'd at least wanted to ask her, disappointment that he never had, confusion as to why. "I know," Arlie said. "But I'm a big girl now. We're both adults. They need a food stylist, I need a job. It's a simple business transaction. The end."

Kassidy took a step toward her, the familiar scent of vanilla and violets blooming as she looked down at Arlie. Even when they were both wearing heels, Kassidy could rest her chin on the crown of Arlie's head.

"All I'm saying is, be careful."

"Careful is the only option I have," Arlie said.

She meant it.

With her parents gone, and her reputation in smoldering tatters, her job at Kane Foods International was all that stood between her and ruin.

Which was why she'd lied to get it.

"Good." Slipping past her to click on the steamer plugged in behind the counter, Kassidy unzipped a gray garment bag to reveal a stunning cream silk gown. "So when do you start?"

"Officially, Monday. Unofficially, tonight. Mason invited me to some kind of investor orgy on the Kane yacht."

"Mason Kane." A dreamy smile smoothed out Kassidy's features as she paused, the wand billowing steam like smoke from a dragon's nostrils. "Now there's the twin *I* would have picked. His scores on standardized tests notwithstanding."

*"You?"* Arlie asked incredulously. "And Mason Kane?"

"You'd be surprised what the love of a good woman can do." Kassidy raised an eyebrow in her haughty *sovereign addressing her subjects* expression. "Along with very clear instructions."

"Speaking of Mason," Arlie said, "I'm supposed to meet him at the Corinthian Yacht Club at six o'clock. Which is why I'm here. I need to borrow a *I definitely belong on a yacht* dress."

"And here I thought it was to apologize for your horrifyingly substandard performance in the best friend department." Kassidy teased.

"Totally that too." Arlie aimed her best disarming smile at her. "Can you help me?"

Kassidy let out an exasperated laugh. "'Can you help me?' she says." Dropping the steaming wand into its holster, she took a step backward to assess Arlie with narrowed eyes. "Six petite," she diagnosed. *"Barely.* Promise me you're going to eat something on that damn boat."

Indeed, Arlie's appetite had evaporated along with her paycheck. Not that she would have spent money in her favorite gourmet food store even if she'd had it. "Scout's honor," she said.

"I've got just the thing." Her friend disappeared behind the curtain and reappeared a few minutes later holding aloft a garment bag that she hung on the hook next to the gown she'd been steaming. With the fanfare usually reserved for ribbon cuttings, she drew down the zipper and shook out the dress with a flourish. "Ta-da!"

Arlie had to stifle a gasp.

In a color somewhere between blush and dusty rose,

the back-bearing, halter-neck bodice dipped low in the front and nipped in at the waist. The skirt, comprised of asymmetrical layers of fluttery chiffon, was both ethereal and earthy. One stiff breeze and there would be a whole lotta leg.

"Oh, Kassidy," Arlie breathed.

"Halston," Kassidy said, running an admiring hand down the length of the skirt. "A concept garment for their 1972 spring line. Basically, the unicorn of cocktail dresses. I found it at an estate sale for a rich as shit socialite who corked off after freak complications with a routine liposuction."

Arlie grinned at her. "It's perfect."

"You're goddamn right it is." Brusquely zipping the garment bag, Kassidy laid it over the counter.

"Shouldn't I try it on?" Arlie asked.

"No need." Kassidy breezed over to a wall at the back of the shop where shoes were arranged in an impressive tiered display. "You still wear a size seven?"

"Yes, but—"

"These." She held aloft a pair of sparkling highheeled strappy sandals.

Arlie briefly considered protesting but thought better of it. "I can't thank you enough."

"I don't need thanks," Kassidy said, her eyes serious as she handed over the garment bag and the silky shoebox. "I need you not to disappear on me ever again."

"No more disappearing." Arlie hooked the dress's hanger over her wrist and tucked the shoebox under her arm. "I promise."

"Good." Leaning against the counter, Kassidy tapped on the screen of an iPad propped in a chrome stand. "I expect a full report of the evening's events."

"As you wish." After a curtsy and a bow, Arlie turned toward the door.

"Banks!" Kassidy called after her.

Already in the doorway, Arlie looked back. "Your Honor?"

"Whatever you do," her friend said, skewering her with the full force of her unnervingly perceptive gaze, "don't kiss him."


With its sharp prow and the streamlined grace of a shark, the *Dolce Vita IV* appeared to be knifing through the water even when standing perfectly still. Its hull was the color of the sky just before dawn. Above it, elegant white decks stacked upon each other in graduating tiers like a wedding cake. On each of them, people had begun to congregate in social clumps.

Music from an old-fashioned brass band floated down the ramp to the yacht, along with a tinkle of high-pitched feminine laughter that dumped ice water down Arlie's spine.

She *knew* that laugh.

Arlie froze, as if she, and not the yacht, were anchored.

Not *her*. Not *here*. This couldn't be happening. What could *she* possibly be doing here?

Arlie looked around at the people moving past her.

No one had spotted her yet. She could turn around right now and sprint back to her car within five minutes. Three, if she lost the medieval torture devices on her feet. She could make apologies via a polite email. Claim car trouble. Or anything to avoid taking another step toward the emotional equivalent of the *Titanic*.

"And I thought *I* was late." The teasing, effervescently masculine voice of Mason Kane lapped at her like a warm wave.

He approached with arms outstretched, a puckish grin on his face. The sunset light caught the crests of his dark hair, casting his tanned skin in the most flattering of glows. He had lost his tie and shucked the sleeves of his beautifully cut button-down shirt to the elbows. Casual in the perfectly arranged way only the deeply wealthy seemed capable of achieving.

"You are," Arlie said, managing a watery smile. "And so am I."

Mason's grin widened. Talented in the art of flirting as he clearly had become, Arlie didn't miss the quick flick of those golden green eyes over her face, her hair, which was released from its chignon prison for the evening, her bare shoulders, her dress.

"Shall we?" he asked, offering her his arm.

Glancing at the yacht, Arlie calculated the odds that she could refuse Mason's offer.

They weren't good.

Looping her arm with his, she climbed the red-carpeted ramp and arrived into a whoosh of conversation and music, a world of lacquered wood, gleaming brass, and gowns and teeth glittering like diamonds beneath a sky turning from sherbet orange to flamingo pink.

Mason snagged two glasses of champagne from the silver tray presented by a waiter with the cleft chin of a soap opera hero.

"Cheers," Mason said, handing the elegant flute to Arlie before clinking its rim with his. "To your future with Kane Foods International."

Arlie, praying her shaking hand wouldn't slosh the drink onto her dress, brought the glass to her lips and took a swallow. Citrusy aromas burst onto her palate, the densely carbonated liquid bringing tears to her eyes. It had been a hot minute since she'd had the good stuff.

Expecting Mason to abandon her any moment for one of the clearly purebred debutantes taking up every available space, Arlie was surprised when he remained at her elbow as she gingerly began to clear the cluster at the top of the entry ramp.

"So, should I begin the introductions, or would you rather make your way through that glass first?" Mason eyed the dainty stem of the champagne glass that Arlie hadn't realized she'd been white-knuckle clutching.

She took another sip and attempted a casual laugh. "Maybe half the glass?"

"Fair enough," Mason agreed, mirroring her healthy swallow. "It's a lot to take in if you're not used to it."

For the second time that evening, she found herself surprised by his display of empathy. A quality he had seemed to altogether lack all the years of their mutual acquaintance growing up.

"You're right about that." Scanning the bottom deck, her shoulders lowered by a couple inches when *she* was nowhere to be seen. If only Arlie's luck would last.

Another uncomfortably attractive server approached them with hors d'oeuvres, the scent wafting up from the tray making Arlie's salivary glands clench uncomfortably. She hadn't been able to force down a single swallow of food since her morning coffee, her nerves having made her mouth into a sand trap and her stomach into a dusty cavern.

When she trained her vision on the haphazardly scattered pile of perfectly baked mini beef Wellingtons, she felt a clench of an entirely different variety.

This tray needed something green to set off the filet's succulent and perfectly pink interior. Resiny sprigs of rosemary or a tangle of freshly snipped sage. A tumble of peppery arugula.

And the arrangement was *all* wrong. Small, decadent pieces like this begged for some kind of contrasting order to emphasize their golden pastry's perfect imperfection.

Her neck ached for the familiar feeling of the wide leather strap, the solid weight of the camera like a security blanket against her chest.

But it was more than that.

The world felt a much safer place when condensed into the small vignette of a lens. In that small space, life could be arranged exactly as she willed it.

"Miss?" The server smiled at her politely.

Arlie took the cocktail napkin and relieved the tray of the bite nearest her. Mason once again followed suit, popping his hors d'oeuvre whole into his mouth and chewing appreciatively. "Not half as good as your mother's," he said, his muscular jaw working. "But not half bad all the same."

Chewing her own bite, Arlie was forced to agree.

After all, it had been her mother who'd patiently explained how colors opposite on the color wheel enhanced each other when placed side by side.

"We eat with our eyes first," her sweet, practical mother had said, wiping her hands on her apron before placing a leafy bunch of sage next to a perfectly bronzed capon. "Never forget that."

Arlie never had.

Just as she'd never forgotten the special scraps her

mother had always saved for her and the kitchen staff. Scooby snacks, she'd called them.

"I'm surprised you remember," Arlie said, washing the last of her Wellington down with a swallow of nostril-tickling champagne. "That was such a long time ago."

"I have a long memory when it comes to food," he said, a killer grin producing that familiar dimple in his cheek. "And women."

"Oh, I remember." With the glass of champagne half gone, Arlie felt the familiar sting of that intoxicating contentment that proximity to luxury so effortlessly wrought.

"Marlowe!" Mason boomed enthusiastically.

Mason and Samuel's ethereally elegant sister approached them, her body expertly draped in a dress the precise aqua-green of sea ice.

"You're looking especially lovely this evening." Mason squeezed his younger sister's yoga-toned bicep before planting a kiss on her cheek.

"I heard a rumor you were joining us." Marlowe's smile didn't quite reach her eyes, pale blue like her father's. Her hair, on the other hand, belonged entirely to her mother. Pale, straight, and nearly platinum, it framed her face in a sleek chin-length bob. "Arlie Banks, this is Neil Campbell, my fiancé."

Neil Campbell had dark hair, all-American features, and eyes just a hair too close together. Which, apparently, didn't prevent them from stealing a grabby glance at Arlie's cleavage before making their leisurely passage upward. If Marlowe noticed this, she gave no indication.

"Pleasure to meet you," Arlie lied, taking his offered hand.

"Likewise." He said this often, judging by the way it rolled smoothly off his tongue.

"Where's Samuel?" Mason asked, scanning the crowd.

Marlowe rolled her eyes and jerked her chin over her shoulder. "Guess."

Mason's chuckle held a curious mix of amusement and brotherly exasperation. "He *would* find the only group of people who look like they're enjoying themselves even less than he is."

Arlie's stomach flipped as she followed his line of sight, where a chance parting of bodies afforded her a sudden view of Samuel Kane, still in his tie and jacket, surrounded by a group of solemn-faced men in similar states of formality.

She wasn't sure if it was the champagne, or a dizzying rush of déjà vu, but Arlie felt herself a little unsteady on her borrowed shoes.

Samuel standing in the corner stiff as a scarecrow at the sprawling party the night of their high school graduation. Back straight, shoulders rigid. Face equally devoid of emotion, wearing his suit coat long after girls had begun kicking off their shoes and boys had begun draping their ties and jackets over the nearest priceless antique.

Then, as now, his tie had been deliberately loosened, the knot falling about two inches away from the precise intersection of his starched collar.

Which Arlie knew with heartbreaking clarity was as relaxed as Samuel could allow himself to be.

And damned if she wasn't seized by the inexplicable urge to yank that tie away, shuck his coat from him, and send every last button on his tailored shirt scattering across the lacquered wood deck there and then.

As if plucking her thoughts from the very air, Samuel stopped midsentence, his eyes locking with hers as the world and everyone in it slipped into a rare pocket of silence interrupted only by the thunderous beating of Arlie's own heart.

Warmth that had nothing to do with the champagne spilled through her, pooling low in her belly. *Samuel Kane had wanted to take her to the prom.*

Silly that she, a grown woman with a multitude of problems on her plate, should still be obsessing about this fact hours after she'd found out. It was a just a high school dance, after all.

But it was what it *meant*.

Once upon a time, shy Samuel, strenuous avoider of direct human contact at all costs, had liked her enough to pluck up the courage to seek out her best friend's advice.

Arlie felt a small stab of triumph as Samuel blinked, abruptly turning to the men waiting for his attention.

"Should we go rescue him from the investment bankers bending his ear about Project Impact?" Mason asked, drawing her attention back to the conversation.

"He doesn't look like he especially wants to be rescued," Arlie said, swearing she could see the faintest hint of crimson flush beneath Samuel's sharp cheekbones.

"Which is exactly why we should do it." Mason treated her to his pirate's smirk.

Feeling an inexplicable magnetic pull somewhere behind her belly button, Arlie gazed up at Mason. "Okay."

# Four

Samuel needed to break something.

Quickly.

Standing before him, a group of investors with the power to change the future of Kane Foods forever vied for his attention. He'd been courting them for over a year at his father's insistence. Ski excursions in Aspen. Fishing trips in Key West. High-roller weekends in Vegas.

After all that work, here they were offering him everything he'd ever wanted, and he wasn't listening to a single thing they were saying.

Because of *her*.

Because of that dress.

Because of the torture that was Arlie Banks.

Samuel had stolen greedy glances as she'd moved through the crowd with Mason at her side, looking every bit the golden god. His brother procuring her champagne. His brother touching his glass to hers. Samuel had nearly bit through his tongue when Mason leaned in, whispering something that caused Arlie to erupt into a spontaneous burst of laughter that vacuumed ten years from her face.

He'd watched as, together, they'd made their way to Marlowe's side, his brother's hand at the small of Arlie's back. Then, just as Samuel had been both terribly pleased his plan was working and quietly dying inside, Arlie had looked right at him.

Not with the kind of darting, nervous glances she'd managed in his office that morning.

*Really* looked at him. No, not just *at* him.

*Into* him.

Like she knew him. Like she knew something *about* him.

A look that shot straight through to his soul by way of his cock.

"Are you quite all right?" Henry Campbell, father of his sister's fiancé asked, his posh British accent revealing none of the tension his face displayed.

"Apologies," Samuel said, desperately sifting his short-term memory for any scrap of conversation he could respond to. "I'm afraid I missed that."

With his beady eyes, rounded belly, and dark gray suit, Campbell looked like nothing so much as an offended pigeon. "I said, I spoke with your father and we're ready to move forward, but—"

*But.*

But the breeze came and Samuel's head instinctively swiveled back toward Arlie, watching as the panels of fabric of her dress parted, revealing the pale length of her thigh.

A thigh he could easily imagine hooked over his hip as he tasted her mouth, pushing her panties aside so he could—

"If your attentions are needed elsewhere, we can certainly discuss our investment in the Kane Foods gummies division another time." Now Henry Campbell didn't just look piqued, he looked pissed. The team of yuppie lackeys welded to his bespoke coattails mirrored his look of refined displeasure.

*What the hell am I doing?*

"Forgive me." He did his best to drag his attention away from the lurid scene he couldn't seem to banish from the screen of his mind. "While we're certainly excited to have Campbell Capital as a partner, I'm sure you're aware how…*attached* my father is to our gummies division. It was the very first automated line in the original Kane Confectionary building. Once we've arrived at a reasonable arrangement where equity is concerned—"

"A *reasonable* arrangement?" Campbell raised an eyebrow. "I thought the percentage we discussed at our last due diligence call was more than generous."

A predatory thrill coursed through Samuel's veins.

He loved this part.

Reading his adversary. Learning their weaknesses. Figuring out exactly where and how to apply the proper pressure to get what he wanted.

Because he always did.

"Well, it would be, if your data analysts hadn't wildly undervalued the division's recurring revenue streams,"

Samuel said, reveling in Campbell's obvious discomfiture.

He was a man not used to being on the defensive.

"Gentlemen." This one word, delivered in Mason's overly affected *listen to how charming I am* voice, had Samuel's hands tightening into fists. "May I borrow my brother?"

Even without turning, he knew Arlie was with him. If the acute, electric tingling at the base of his spine wasn't evidence enough, the appreciative gleam in the eyes of Campbell and his cronies as they looked past Samuel would have been a dead giveaway.

"We're in the middle of a discussion, Mason. Can't this wait?" he snapped.

"No," Mason said, folding his arms over his chest, his skin a tanning-bed bronze against the pristine white of his dress shirt. "I'm afraid it can't."

With a heavy sigh, Samuel addressed the entourage. "Gentlemen, can we revert offline?"

"Of course." Campbell nodded curtly before shuffling off into the crowd, his loyal satellites trailing in his wake.

Once they were gone, Samuel focused his full attention on his brother, doing his best not to look at Arlie, who hovered behind his shoulder like a golden ghost. "What is it?"

Mason beamed an infuriatingly jovial grin. "I thought you might like to introduce Miss Banks to some of our team. Seeing as you are our chief executive officer."

Samuel's jaw tightened. "You seemed like you were doing a perfectly fine job."

"I'm afraid my attentions are needed urgently at the bar."

Arlie and Samuel both followed the direction of his gaze, where a small congregation of leggy, laughing ladies were worshipping the god of Frosé.

Resentment oozed in Samuel's gut. As he had with so many assignments before, Mason wanted to hand off the single task he'd been given for the evening.

Clearly, more careful orchestrations throwing Arlie and Mason together would be required.

"Fine," Samuel said.

*"Miss Banks."* Mason bowed, imitating Samuel's formality from her interview this morning.

They stood there facing each other after Mason's departure, the twelve years that had elapsed evaporating as Samuel morphed into the helplessly tongue-tied teenager he had always been in her presence. He desperately tried to remind himself of the models he'd bedded, the companies he'd bought and sold, the billions he'd made.

All of it reduced to a heap of ash by her shy smile.

"You really don't have to," Arlie said preemptively. "Introduce me around, that is. I know that inviting me to come tonight was kind of Mason's idea."

"Yes," he said. "It was." *After Samuel had suggested it to him.*

"Those were investment bankers?"

Samuel watched as Arlie sipped from the champagne flute, the knuckles of her hand white, her lips flushed a vivid raspberry-red.

"Yes," he answered, trying not to think of how she'd taste if he kissed her at that precise moment.

"And the negotiations are going well?" she asked.

"So far."

"Are you seeking funding for the nutrition and wellness division expansion that you mentioned this morning?" The question was labored, her tone edged with conversational desperation.

Seeing Arlie's eyes etched with discomfort he knew he'd caused, Samuel felt compelled to slam his head against the nearest state cabin door.

He wanted to tell her everything.

To tell her how, when they were teenagers, he would write out lists of conversation starters, only to find himself completely helpless every time she entered the room. To explain that, in college, he'd forced himself into every public speaking and debate class his heavily loaded schedule could handle, simply to learn how to speak to other humans. To practice making the vivid world in his head manifest through words. He wished he could show her how hard he had tried not to be as tongue-tied as he was now.

Instead, he settled for, "Yes."

Arlie's lush mouth flattened into an irritated line. Draining the last swallow of her champagne, she plunked it without ceremony on the empty tray of a passing waiter.

"Look," she said. "I'm exceedingly grateful for the opportunity to work for Kane Foods, but it's obvious you don't particularly want me here tonight. I'm not particularly thrilled either, but here we are. We can either pretend to have a conversation, or I can excuse myself and get the hell off this boat. Which will it be?"

Anger darkened her irises from cobalt to sapphire, her cheeks flushing beneath the flaxen waves that Samuel longed to drag his fingers through.

"You can't," he said.

"Oh, believe me, I can." Raising herself to the full height on heels Samuel had been imagining fastened behind his neck, Arlie aimed a challenging gaze up at him.

"No." Samuel inclined his head, jerking his chin toward the red-carpeted dock behind her. "You can't."

The *Dolce Vita* had set sail.

Despite the stab of fear tightening her stomach, Arlie pasted an artificially bright smile on her face before turning back to Samuel. "Well, I guess you're going to have to talk to me then."

At that precise moment, Mason's hearty laugh rose above the general throng, followed by a chorus of female tittering.

Someone who had spent less time studying Samuel might have missed the subtle hardening of his features. "It appears so."

Flagging down a passing server, Arlie retrieved another flute of champagne.

"For you, sir?" the server asked, looking to Samuel.

"No, thank you."

"Isn't that the whole point of these corporate mixers?" Arlie asked. "To make the company more tolerable with booze?" She took a demonstrative sip of her drink.

"It dulls the senses and loosens the tongue. An exceedingly unfortunate choice in circumstances such as these."

"Something tells me you could use an unfortunate choice or two." Arlie bit her tongue almost as quickly as the words left it. What in God's name was she thinking?

"Arlie Banks!"

Panic sent her intestines skittering about twelve inches to the south.

It was *her*.

Taegan Lynch. Gossip. Busybody. Director of marketing at *Gastronomie*. The one and only person besides her former boss and the editorial director who knew exactly why Arlie had been let go from her previous position.

Steeling her spine, Arlie watched Taegan sauntering toward her. Toward *them*.

Her face was difficult to read, but then, copious Botox and other assorted fillers could to that to a person. Glossy dark brown hair spilled over her shoulders, framing the deep swell of her cleavage. The bleached white teeth of her beauty queen smile beamed between collagen-enhanced lips.

Her slim, lithe pantsuit-clad form slithered over to them, Louboutin heels beating an alarming staccato rhythm on the expensive wood deck.

Arlie watched Samuel, hoping to God that she wouldn't see in him the kind of unabashed lust Taegan seemed to evoke in every single male member of the population.

What she saw was curiosity and careful assessment. Exceedingly dangerous. Especially considering the first thing he did after looking at Taegan was to aim the engine of his analysis back at Arlie.

Very bad.

Very, very bad.

"What on earth are you doing on this boat?" Taegan smacked a kiss sticky with gloss on each of Arlie's cheeks.

She resisted the urge to wipe them off with the backs of her hands. "I could ask you the same."

Taegan looked over at Samuel. "I'm a guest of Parker

Kane this evening. He reached out about doing a feature on the Willow Creek Winery in the fall issue of *Gastronomie*." Taegan glanced back and forth between her and Samuel, clearly inviting her to make an introduction.

"Taegan Lynch, this is Samuel Kane, CEO of—"

"Oh, I know *exactly* who he is," Taegan purred. "Parker insisted that I come over and introduce myself. But if I'm interrupting…" she trailed off, daring Arlie to try and stop her.

"Not at all," Samuel said. "Miss Banks and I were just catching up. She just joined our team as senior food stylist."

"Is that so?" Taegan's smile took on a carnivorous edge. "Well, you're certainly getting a very talented resource. I know we were all just heartbroken when she left so suddenly."

Arlie's cheeks prickled as the blood drained from her face. Night air chilled the sudden sweat that had bloomed on the back of her neck.

"In fact, would you mind if I borrowed her for just a moment?" Taegan asked in a voice that suggested sugar wouldn't melt on her tongue.

Samuel flicked a glance in her direction, a subtle but unmistakable question in his eyes.

*Did she want him to go?*

As tempted as she was to send a pleading *please don't let her take me* look in reply, Arlie was afraid of the conclusions he might draw if she did. She nodded in assent.

"I suppose I've monopolized Miss Banks's time long enough. Pleasure to meet you," Samuel said with a polite nod in Taegan's direction before disappearing into the crowd.

"Shall we?" Looping her arm through Arlie's like an old friend, Taegan steered them toward an unoccupied sofa overlooking the yacht's back deck.

Arlie accompanied her on wooden legs, the sound of conversations around them muffled by the roaring of blood in her ears.

Taegan seated herself, motioning for Arlie to do the same.

Though she would have far preferred to hurl herself over the deck railing at that precise moment, Arlie perched stiffly on the edge of the sofa cushion.

"Because I know how much you'd like to rejoin your coworkers, I'll get straight to the point."

"Please do," Arlie said, trying to keep her expression neutral despite the polar vortex of fear spiraling in her chest.

"I take it the Kanes are unaware of the circumstances of your departure from *Gastronomie*?" Crossing one long leg over the other, Taegan rotated the pointed toe of her tan patent leather heel.

Arlie's heart sank. She had known this was coming. Had felt it in some deep, primordial place the second she'd heard Taegan's laugh like the tinkling of broken glass on the evening air. "You are correct."

"And I suppose you'd like to keep it that way?" Taegan arched an artfully shaped eyebrow at her.

The tangle of conversations and music had taken on a shrill edge, as if Arlie were in a disaster movie in that split second before the world began to tip off its axis. "What is it that you want?"

A feline smile leisurely unfurled itself on Taegan's face. "Information."

Acid crawled up from a stomach that felt hot and sick. "What kind of information?"

"It's come to my attention that Kane Foods is planning on branching into the nutritional and wellness space. Seeing as how you're adept at *accidentally* gathering confidential information and obviously chummy with Samuel Kane, I thought you might be able give me a little preview of what they have planned."

"Why would that be relevant to *Gastronomie* ?"

"That's none of your concern." Taegan lifted her wine to her lips, the ruby liquid dancing against the sides of the glass. "Only how you're going to get me what I need."

"I'm afraid I can't do that," Arlie said. "I signed an NDA."

"Oh, Arlie." Taegan smiled and laid a hand over hers in a way that would look to anyone else like she'd said something fantastically funny. "That certainly didn't stop you last time."

Arlie looked up in time to catch Samuel briefly glancing in her direction.

"Taegan, please." Arlie didn't so much say the words as force them from her mouth. "I don't expect you to understand this, but I'm not entirely sure you actually know what happened between me and Hugh."

Her stomach clenched at the sound of his name. The charismatic marketing executive of a rival magazine, he had wined and dined her under the premise of a potential job offer only to mine her for information that landed her in the crosshairs of a corporate espionage lawsuit.

"I don't need to." Setting her wineglass on the side table, Taegan brushed a tendril of hair away from her cheekbone. "I just need you to be useful."

Arlie leaned in, dropping her voice to a confidential level. "I'm not going to be useful in any way that compromises Samuel's project."

Taegan's hyena laugh raised the fine hairs on Arlie's arms. "As ironic as I find your misguided loyalty, it might ease your conscience to know Samuel Kane is even more ruthless than his father in business matters."

Anger boiled beneath Arlie's skin, her hands tightening into fists next to her hips.

"No, he's not."

"Oh, really?" Taegan smiled widely. "Ask him about Millhaven Foods. Family-run, not terribly sophisticated. Acquired for significantly less than they were worth. Dismantled. An entire family legacy destroyed."

It was a pattern Arlie knew all too well.

"They had none other than Samuel Kane to thank," Taegan continued. "I understand he's exceedingly persuasive when pursuing something he wants."

By all rights, this statement shouldn't have sent an illicit thrill surging through her.

"Things like that happen in every industry," Arlie said. "That doesn't mean—"

"I don't know why you're pretending like you have a choice here." Taegan inclined her head, stroking the stem of her discarded wine glass. "Unless…you'd like me to walk over to Samuel right now and tell him what I know."

Together, they looked in his direction.

Surrounded by men whose postures were quickly

becoming booze-loose and slouchy, Samuel still stood like he had a javelin welded to his spine.

As if sensing her gaze on his back, he turned his head, his strong chin angled over his shoulder, his eyes alert and assessing.

Samuel might have taken her apparent acceptance of Taegan's request for a chat, but he had remained *aware* of them ever since.

Arlie imagined Taegan sauntering over to him, how his features would shift when the words registered. How his eyes would go black and empty like a shark's.

"Provided I were able to get the information you want," Arlie said, "how exactly would you intend to use it?"

"Let's just say that I'm in contact with a company that would come to market with a certain product before Kane Foods saturates the market. It would be a life-changing event for all its employees. For Kane Foods, it would barely be a blip on the radar. No more than a cat scratch." Taegan shrugged.

Arlie's eyes narrowed. "But it wouldn't come back on Samuel Kane?"

Taegan scooted closer to her, a mocking smirk twisting her lips. "You seem awfully invested in his interests for a brand new employee. Is there something I should know?"

"Promise me," Arlie said, ignoring the question.

"I promise." Taegan held out her hand.

Arlie stared at it for the space of several heartbeats then shook, immediately feeling like she needed to wash her hand afterward.

"Well," Taegan sighed, pushing herself up from the

sofa. "I'm glad we were able to reach an understanding. I look forward to a mutually beneficial partnership."

Two hours later, Arlie's cheeks hurt from forced smiles and her stomach protested its total neglect since the lone piece of beef Wellington she'd been able to get down. Seeking self-preserving solitude, she had snuck away from the crowd and escaped down the back stairs used by the catering staff.

Her kind of people, after all.

Blessedly alone on the bottom deck at the stern of the yacht, she watched the full moon's reflection shimmer on the waves in the motor's churning wake.

Arlie felt herself unraveling. The anxiety she'd battled all evening returned to her in a vicious gust. Her lungs refused to fill with air despite her rapid, panting breaths as her whole body began to shake. Tears stung her eyes and she bit her lip to keep them from overflowing and spilling down her cheeks. Gripping the silky wooden railing, she fought to compose herself.

She couldn't do this here.

She couldn't do this now.

"Strange night."

Gasping, Arlie whirled around, squinting into the darkness. Through the pocket of blue-black shadow, she could just make out a man seated alone on the leather bench, a rocks glass of amber liquid in his hand.

Samuel.

He leaned forward, his patrician profile unmistakable against the backlit window behind him.

She drew in a long, slow breath of the cooling night air and turned to lean on the railing. "I thought you didn't drink at these functions," she said, trying to sound more casual than she felt.

Ice rattled as he swirled the glass's contents. "Tonight is an exception."

She heard him rise, his solitary footfalls on the deck as he approached her.

Warmth draped itself over her shoulders, the sudden and unexpected comfort startling her.

He had given her his coat.

Arlie shifted, as much to feel the silky lining of the jacket still warmed by his body heat on her skin as to make sure she hadn't just dreamed this. Tilting her chin, she rubbed the edge of her jaw on the coat's collar, his scent filling her nostrils. Soap and skin. Cotton and subtle cologne.

"Thank you," she said.

He came up beside her, stooping to lean on the railing that came to the bottom of Arlie's breasts. They stood side by side looking out over the river, elbows barely touching, that single point of contact becoming the axis of Arlie's awareness.

"I've made many unfortunate choices, by the way," Samuel said, picking up the thread of their earlier conversation. He brought the glass to his lips and sipped.

Feeling the weight of all that implied, Arlie remembered Taegan's earlier comments. *More ruthless than his father.*

"If you're speaking of your and Mason's sixteenth birthday party," Arlie began, a film reel of memories already unspooling on the screen of her mind, "you shouldn't worry. I don't think anyone remembers what happened that night especially well."

Now that was a bold-faced lie.

If any single image persisted to this day, it was Samuel Kane naked beneath the full moon.

Self-conscious and godlike all at once. His perfect dive into dark water. Coming up right next to her, the first spray of his exhilarated exhale landing on her cheeks and wet hair. The scent of it more intoxicating than the pilfered whiskey they'd been passing around on that long, hot summer night.

Which was precisely the point at which he'd realized that, contrary to what Mason had told him, no one else had taken off their bathing suits.

"I'm not," Samuel said, those sensuous lips tightening into a displeased line. "And I would prefer to never again."

"Don't be so hard on yourself." Arlie gripped the wood railing. "I don't think anyone's first experience with whiskey ends well."

"Actually…" He slid her a secretive, sideways glance. "That may not have been my *first* experience with whiskey."

"Is that so?" Arlie feigned an air of scandalized disbelief.

An entire ship full of investors and potential acquisition targets, and here they were, discussing high school hijinks.

Her heart fluttered like a nervous bird. Samuel Kane was talking to her.

To *her*.

How often had she laid in her narrow single bed, the princess canopy above her a dream catcher for feverish teenage fantasies of just this sort?

A passing gust of wind teased the hair from Arlie's

neck. Sailboats skimmed across the river around them, their white sails like the fins of overgrown sharks.

"My father used to hide the keys to his liquor cabinet," Samuel said.

*My father.*

Arlie had to work to listen to the rest of the sentence after these two words. At this casual mention of the man who had destroyed her mother's life and, by extension, their family.

"Did he?" she asked a beat too late.

"He did," Samuel said. "Imagine my surprise when I found them in his hollowed-out copy of Machiavelli's *The Prince*. Naturally, I was curious."

"Naturally," Arlie mimicked. "What did you do?"

A rare, soul-warming smile spreading across his lips. "Research." He paused and cocked his head. Then his hand slowly moved toward her face.

For one fleeting moment, Arlie imagined it coming to rest on her jaw, guiding her mouth toward his until the unaccountable geography of their lips aligned. Something heavy and molten spilled through her middle as she realized that she wanted this.

Wanted it badly.

"Eyelash." Samuel's thumb grazed her cheekbone. "Make a wish."

Gazing up into emerald eyes full of nostalgia and moonlight, stars scattered like diamonds on a bolt of sapphire velvet overhead, Arlie was utterly and completely helpless to stop the words from tumbling out of her mouth.

"I wish I had known you wanted to take me to prom."

# Five

Samuel Kane could count on one hand the times he'd been truly surprised.

He made it his business to anticipate every possible person and event with the power to affect his life and spent a great deal of time developing contingency plans for just such occasions.

He hadn't planned for this moment.

And now here he was, his mouth hanging open, blinking like twelve years of his life had evaporated and his seventeen-year-old self stood facing Arlie Banks.

Arlie plucked the glass from his hand without invitation and took a swallow. Samuel tried—and failed—not to imagine the channel of heat spreading on her tongue and sliding like silk down her throat.

"After our meeting this morning, I went to see Kassidy Nichols. My best friend from high school?"

Sifting through his memory, Samuel uncovered only the shallowest recollection of her image.

"When I told her that I was coming to work at Kane Foods, she mentioned that once upon a time you had asked her advice about taking me to prom." She paused, awaiting confirmation.

"I did," he admitted, steeling himself for the inevitable follow-up question.

"Why didn't you?"

The part of him dedicated to deflecting pain at all costs supplied a ready defense.

*I knew you hadn't been asked and I felt sorry for you.*

He could say this right now. He could end this conversation and send her scurrying away from him tonight and forever.

He might have, if not for what he'd seen earlier.

The look on Arlie's face the second she'd heard Taegan Lynch's voice. Her entire body had tensed and before she'd had a chance to rearrange her features, he'd seen genuine fear in the depths of her eyes.

So thick, he could almost taste it.

It had taken every ounce of his considerable restraint not to scoop Arlie off her feet, throw her cavemanstyle over his shoulder, and carry her away from general vicinity.

Not that such overblown displays of romanticism had ever been within his purview.

He'd only read about them.

"I chickened out," he said. A huge understatement of the roughly seventy-eight times he'd hovered in her vicinity, rehearsing what he'd say only to have the words evaporate when he took a step in her direction. They were quiet as a sloop sailed past, the cozy family aboard gathered around a table on the deck.

"I would have said yes." Arlie took another sip from his glass before handing it back to him.

The rim was still warm and wet from her mouth. A smoky communion between them. "Why is that?"

She leaned forward on the railing, her cascade of blond waves almost silver in the moonlight. "I liked you."

This was why he never drank around other people. In his current state, he was altogether unequipped to deal with this revelation.

Everything he couldn't say burned at the base of his throat. *I liked you too. You were warm, and kind, and the first person who wasn't charmed by my brother.*

His brother.

The whole reason Arlie Banks was on this boat in the first place. Would she be making such admissions if she knew Samuel's real secret?

What remained of his logical mind warned him that he was in imminent danger of derailing his plan, but he found himself physically incapable of saying words that would wound her further. Words that would send her flying into his brother's arms for comfort.

The simple, logical explanation he'd been battling since the moment she'd walked into his office had crystalized when he'd watched from the darkness, her narrow shoulders slumped, her body shaking.

*He* wanted to comfort her.

He wanted her in his arms.

He wanted her in his bed.

What terrible irony it was, discovering the glar-

ingly unexpected flaw in his own plan. By hiring Arlie
Banks, he hadn't just made her forbidden for Mason.

He'd made her forbidden for himself.

Such exquisite torture, to stand next to her in the
wake of her admission. To drink in her sexy smirk and
to know she could never be his.

"The way I see it, I owe you a dance," she said as
she gazed at the upper deck, where music had begun
playing and the crowd had sorted itself into pairs hit-
ting the makeshift dance floor.

Arlie stole his glass once again, setting it on a nearby
table, then shrugged off the suit coat he had draped over
her shoulders and slung it across the back of an adjacent
chair. He experienced a sympathetic twitch, exposed as
he was, desperately wanting the familiar weight of it
back on his shoulders.

Sliding her small, cold hands into his large warm
ones, she tugged him toward a patch of deck beneath a
crisscrossing ideogram of twinkling string lights.

Arlie nodded approvingly. "It's no *I Left My Heart
in San Francisco*, but it will do."

Samuel blinked at her, hoping he reflected an appropriate approximation of puzzlement. "Was that the
prom theme?" he asked, knowing full well that it was.

She smiled wide enough to reveal the tiny dimple at
the left corner of her mouth. "Décor-wise, yes. Which
you would have known if you'd come."

"And watch you dance with someone else?" he
teased.

"Speaking of dances," she said, her eyebrows gathering at the center of her forehead in an adorably serious
manner. "You have a very important decision to make."

"And that would be?"

"First or last?" she asked.

"Pardon?"

"If we're going to recreate a dance from the prom we never went to together, we need to decide which part of the night we're recreating."

Personally, Samuel preferred the part where they would have fled the Lennox Finch event hall to have sex in the old Packard limo his father would have insisted they take.

Not so his children could enjoy the luxury of riding in it, but so the other guests could see them arriving in it.

"What's the difference?" Though he'd been to a good many black tie benefits and other philanthropic events where dancing had been required, it usually only involved a quick ceremonial sweep around the dance floor with an appropriately well-healed debutante.

"At the beginning of prom, you'd have one hand in mine and the other on my shoulder. By the end, I'd have my arms around your neck and you'd have yours around my waist."

"I'm not so sure about that." Stepping closer to her, he tightened the knot of his tie in an ode to his younger, painfully prim self. "I was a very shy boy."

"True," she said, reaching her delicate fingers up to loosen the knot again. "But I was a very persistent girl."

Their eyes met for a beat of time that seemed to last forever.

"Last," he said.

"Last dance it is." Arlie kicked off her shoes. "I was definitely over these by end of prom."

He let his hands land on the delicate swell of her

hipbones. The warmth of her skin bloomed through the thin, silky fabric, radiating into his palms.

"Who *did* you end up going with?" he asked, trying his best to sound only mildly interested.

Raising an eyebrow at him, Arlie rested her hands over his, guiding them to her lower back.

"Kassidy." Her breasts nudged his ribs as she reached up, lacing her fingers behind his neck as she began to sway in time with the music. "We created quite a stir."

"I'm sure." He began to move with her, his lower back aching with the effort of keeping his hips from grazing hers.

"Do you remember how the Lennox Finch chaperones used to use a King James Bible to measure the distance between couples?" Arlie asked.

"Vaguely. I wasn't big into the social gatherings." To Samuel's irritation, and despite his most strenuous wishes, he felt the telltale heaviness gathering low in his groin. Perfect. He was officially his teenage self again, complete with inconvenient erections.

"But you came to the party after graduation," she said.

*Shit.*

He'd been hoping she wouldn't bring that up.

In those days, he and Mason had looked enough alike that they were frequently mistaken for each other by teachers and friends. Until they opened their mouths.

Mason's mouth had been opened a lot that night.

Tongue-kissing his way through half the senior class, he'd finally made his way over to Arlie, who, for the very first time in their entire teenage career, seemed to be listening attentively to what his brother had to say.

Samuel remembered the stab of panic he'd felt when his brother leaned in, whispering into Arlie's ear before disappearing out the back door of the house where they were illicitly gathered. Just then, their classmate hosting the party announced they would be playing seven minutes in heaven.

Quickly slipping into the small guest bathroom, Samuel had inspected himself in the mirror. He'd then taken off his suit coat and tie, and stowed them away in the linen closet next to a stack of folded washrags before popping the first three buttons on his shirt.

With hands shaking from pure, fizzy adrenaline, he had mussed his hair, turning this way and that to make sure it resembled *Mason's*.

Once the rest of him looked right, he'd removed his glasses, hiding them behind a bottle of designer hand lotion before making his way down the hallway, fingertips trailing along on the wall to orient himself in space.

Luckily, the other partygoers had assumed he was drunk rather than disastrously near-sighted—an unexpected boon in his favor.

A crisply folded fifty tucked into their hostess's palm was all it took for her to magically draw Mason's and Arlie's names from the red plastic cup.

Among a hearty chorus of catcalls and lascivious hooting, they'd made their way into the closet. As soon as the door closed behind them, they were abruptly plunged into inky darkness.

"Is this weird?" she'd asked.

Afraid that words would fail him as they so often had, Samuel had leaned into her instead, until slowly, in an absence of light as primordial as the beginning of the world, they'd found each other in the dark.

Timidly at first, their lips grazed. Warm, dry and velvety, her breath was honey-sweet and hot on his cheeks. Her scent was a gift to the senses left available to him.

Yielding to a need deeper than thirst, his tongue had slid over hers, demanding more. More of this. More of her.

Then he'd found the softness of her breasts beneath her thin cotton blouse. She had moaned into his mouth when he had thumbed her nipple, hard as a pearl. She had pushed his free hand down to the edge of her skirt and beyond, pressing it against the damp heat of the panties between her thighs.

"Please."

This one word had unstitched him. Not because she'd wanted him. Because she had wanted him only when he was pretending to be his brother.

Breaking the kiss, Samuel had drawn back, panting.

For a strange measure of time, he was neither anchored in the past or present, but some muddy fusion of both.

Same sensations.

Different time.

He was back on the deck of the *Dolce Vita*, Arlie Banks in his arms, her eyes wide and her lips swollen and glistening. The hem of her silky dress was drawn up to her waist and his hand was beneath it, coated with the slick warmth of her desire.

His own mouth stung, blood throbbing in his veins, a painful ache in his cock.

What had he done?

"I'm sorry," he said, pulling himself abruptly away from her. "Oh, my God, I'm so sorry. I didn't mean to—"

"All this time." She blinked up at him, eyes dark, pupils dilated with desire as if she had plucked his memories from the very air. "I knew it was you."

# Six

Clearly, she was being punished.

Sitting at the long, lacquered table in the Kane Foods' twenty-fifth-floor executive boardroom, Arlie had listened to herself being officially introduced to the leadership team, the room a blur of names and faces she couldn't possibly remember. All politely nodding to her, offering her warm, welcoming smiles.

All, that is, save one.

Samuel hadn't so much as looked at her since she'd set foot in the room. He sat hunched over, his attention apparently riveted on the leather padfolio open on the table before him like it contained the secrets to life, the universe and everything.

This should have annoyed her. Instead, she felt a twinge of triumph.

No one at this table, not even Parker Kane himself,

knew that less than twelve hours earlier, Samuel Kane's hand had been up her skirt.

And it hadn't been the first time.

Following their closet session, his abrupt departure and stony silence had thwarted any hopes she'd had that the kiss would lead to anything more.

Last night's events had been eerily similar. Samuel had quickly disengaged and bolted without so much as a word, managing to avoid her entirely until the *Dolce Vita IV* had docked a mere thirty minutes later.

After her solo ride home, Arlie had spent a very long, very lonely, night wrestling the sheets in the bed of the apartment that had been part home, part recovery ward in the days since *Gastronomie.* Past and present had braided themselves into a vivid tapestry as the versions of herself separated by twelve years and oceans of pain blurred together.

"Miss Banks?"

Arlie quickly snapped out of her reverie. "Yes?"

"I was saying, we have a tradition here at Kane Foods whenever we welcome a new member aboard." Tanya McKay, vice president of Human Resources, lover of painfully tight ballet buns, cast a nervous glance in Arlie's direction. "It's very simple, really. Just a question that we all answer."

"Of course," Arlie said, hoping she'd be able to cobble together something halfway intelligent on the spot.

"What would you be willing to do to contribute to the success of Kane Foods?"

Glancing down the length of a table that felt half a football field long and probably cost more than any home she'd ever lived in, Arlie was chagrined by the words that left her lips but powerless to stop them. "Anything short of karaoke?"

The swell of appreciative chuckles suffered a quick death when it reached Parker Kane, who was glowering at the head of the table.

"We're very much looking forward to your contributions to the team." Tanya's dark eyes skipping toward Arlie as she pushed a straying hair back into her bun. "Mason spoke very highly of you."

Arlie couldn't help but notice how Samuel tensed at the mention of his brother's name. Just as he had earlier, when their father had made apologies on Mason's behalf.

With his long fingers clutching his Montblanc pen, Samuel looked like he wasn't so much *taking* notes as he was carving them into the creamy paper of his notepad.

She tried not to think of his surprise when she'd told him that she'd always known it wasn't Mason in the closet with her.

He hadn't known that she knew.

"Unless anyone else has any pressing business." The bodies around the table snapped to attention at the resonant sound of the Kane patriarch's voice rolling through the room. "We are adjourned."

All the pompous prick lacked was a gavel.

As everyone filed out of the conference room, Arlie felt a warm hand cup her elbow.

"Congratulations on surviving your first leadership huddle." She was met by the impish grin of Ericka Cheng, VP of Marketing and Mason's second in command. "I know you're probably completely buried in all the brand guidelines I dumped in your lap this morning, but any chance you'd want to go grab coffee?"

With eyeballs still gritty from hours spent fantasizing instead of sleeping, Arlie stole a glance at Samuel quitting the conference room as if the devil himself pursued him with a fiery pitchfork aimed at his perfectly formed ass.

"That's so nice of you." Arlie reached down to gather her planner. "Where did you have in mind?"

"The break room. It just so happens that in addition to being a talented novelist, our own Charlotte Westbrook makes *the* most addictive flat white this side of the Philadelphia River." Ericka looked toward the end of the table, where a silky redhead in a pencil skirt and high-necked blouse paused in her effort to gather up a stack of papers, her cheeks blooming a rabid scarlet.

"Ericka," Charlotte hissed. "You promised not to tell anyone."

"Relax, Charlotte. Arlie is one of us," Ericka said, winking. "And anyway, word of mouth is still the most effective method of marketing, in case I haven't mentioned it."

"You've mentioned it a lot." With a stack of folders and closed laptop hugged against her bosom, Charlotte made her way down the length of the table. From this close vantage, Arlie was free to notice how quietly exquisite the Keeper of Kane Schedules truly was.

Sienna-brown eyes, hair the color of good cabernet piled at the top of her head, lips worthy of print ads, silver cat-shaped earrings swinging from her delicate lobes.

"I would," Ericka said, "if you let me join."

"The very last thing I need is for Parker Kane to know I write spicy novels in the hours I don't spend managing his general existence and otherwise assisting the executive team." Charlotte shifted on her stiletto heels, shouldering her armful of paperwork.

"On the contrary." Ericka reached out and relieved Charlotte of part of her burden. "I'm convinced that reading them would significantly improve his temperament to the benefit of all."

"As much as I'd love to dish," Charlotte said, scratching her shapely calf with the pointy toe of her shoe, "I have expense reports to finish and I haven't even started picking the menus for the awards banquet at Supply Side West. Not to mention coordinating the executive sand dune excursion for the supplier appreciation event in Fort Funston."

"That settles it," Ericka said. "You're having coffee *with* us. Lady bosses gotta stick together."

Charlotte blew a tendril away from her black-framed glasses. "You two are lady bosses. I'm the girl who works for man bosses."

"What have I told you about that kind of limited thinking?" Ericka challenged.

Charlotte made a decidedly unladylike sound.

"Tell me that when you get barked at for bringing Parker Kane coffee in the wrong mug."

"If it were me, he'd be wearing it."

Ericka looked down at her smartwatch. "Give me fifteen minutes to answer a couple emails and then we rendezvous in the kitchen at eleven thirty?"

Arlie glanced at the ornately carved grandfather clock in the corner of the conference room. That would give her time to bolt down the energy drink secreted in her nondesigner purse. "Perfect," she said.

But when she descended ten floors to her brand-new

blank cube of an office, she discovered Samuel Kane waiting for her in it.

Arlie froze in the entryway, the air abruptly vacuumed from her lungs.

Unlike his own palatial floor-to-ceiling windows with their jaw-dropping views, Arlie's office only enjoyed a sliver of daylight, afforded by a vertical window much like those used by medieval archers. Samuel stood facing away from her, hands clasped at the small of his back as he looked out through the narrow rectangle. Today, his armor was a sleek midnight-blue suit.

She hadn't had time to alert him to her presence when he turned, her stomach fluttering when their eyes met.

"Miss Banks," he said with a polite nod.

Though she was sorely tempted to inform him that such formality might not be necessary after his tongue had been in her mouth recently, she suspected that this might not help her cause.

Well, *causes*.

First, keeping her job.

Second, keeping Taegan Lynch off her ass.

Third, keeping herself from leaping into Samuel Kane's Brooks Brothers bedecked lap.

Fourth, keeping her job.

"Mr. Kane," she said, trying to achieve the same tone of cool formality. Forcing her legs to work, Arlie crossed the distance and set her things down on her desk, pretending that she really belonged there. "Please." She motioned toward one of the chairs across from her desk, noticing Samuel's hesitation as he looked at her, then the chair, then at her again.

Arlie had offered the seat as a way of gauging exactly why he'd come. Anything work-related would most likely be delivered while standing. Hasty, awkward, over as soon as possible.

An apology, on the other hand. That, Samuel would definitely want to conduct while sitting opposite her.

He seated himself.

*Shit.*

Arlie did the same.

"I just wanted to…to apologize," he began. "For what happened. On the yacht."

"That?" Arlie laughed, trying to conjure Kassidy's effervescent playfulness. "No apologies needed. I'd already forgotten." She heard the lie leave her lips and instantly hated herself even more.

As if that were possible.

"Oh?" Samuel's eyes flicked from her face to her sparse desk.

Arlie found herself wishing she'd added some personal touches. Some framed pictures of her mother and father. The pithy, ironic paperweight in the shape of a banana that had graced every office she'd occupied. One of the plants she'd hauled home from her previous job under such ignominious circumstances. Anything to keep him from looking at her with that half sorry, half hurt gaze.

"Of course. I mean, if I had a dollar for every whiskey-fueled kiss, I wouldn't even need this job." The laugh that she had meant to sound warm and forgiving came off shrill as a rusty teakettle.

Samuel smoothed the crease in his slacks. "Well, I'm certainly relieved to hear you weren't offended."

"Not in the least. It was an accidental slide down

memory lane. There's nothing to worry about. It didn't mean a thing."

"Not a thing," he agreed.

"Knock, knock." Arlie looked up to see Mason Kane slouching in her doorway, a walking ad for expensive aftershave or top-shelf self-tanner.

Samuel shot out of his chair like his joints had been replaced with springs.

"Sorry to interrupt," Mason said, his ludicrously perfect teeth gleaming in an amused smile. "I was going to borrow *Miss Banks* for a quick cup of coffee."

"You're not interrupting," Samuel said, all elbows and haste. "I was just leaving."

"Oh," Arlie said, thinking of Ericka and Charlotte waiting for her in the break room; she was already five minutes late. "Actually, I was supposed to link up with Ericka Cheng. She wanted to—"

"You know what you two should do," Samuel cut in. "There's a brand-new bistro that opened in the Five Penn Center building. Their espresso is imported directly from Trieste. You should go before *Phillymag* kills it with a rave."

"Since when am I allowed to leave the building on a weekday before noon without receiving a check in the Unforgivable Wastrels column of your little leather notebook?" Mason raised a roguish eyebrow at his clearly flustered brother as he sauntered into the office and slid into the chair his twin had just vacated.

"You make me sound like some kind of tally-taking task master," Samuel said, attempting a casual laugh.

"No effort required on my part." Mason winked at Arlie from across the desk.

Such a strange reversal from a mere four days ago,

with her now behind the desk and the Kane twins in front of it.

"So *this* is why you were a no-show."

Ericka and Charlotte stood in the doorway Mason had evacuated. Ericka with her arms folded across the chest of her chic suit and Charlotte, chewing her lip and staring at her designer shoes.

The only question in Arlie's mind at that particular moment was which of the Kanes Charlotte had a thing for.

One way to find out.

Arlie rose behind her desk. "Gentlemen, my apologies. I promised these two lovely humans I would have coffee with them. Also, Ericka is going to bring me up to speed about the plans for Supply Side West."

Mason unfolded himself from his chair, "I need to catch up with Angela about the very same subject. Why don't I join you?"

Arlie watched as Charlotte's lips tugged upward, the roses returning to her cheeks. "Actually," she said, looking pained, "you're late for an eleven-thirty meeting with Laurel Greaves…the chief commercial officer of Neutratanicals? You've already canceled on him twice."

"Of course." Mason thumped his lineless forehead with a knuckle in mock exasperation. "You know I'd die without you, Charlotte."

Charlotte's cheeks turned an even darker shade of crimson as she watched him exit.

Mason.

She definitely had a thing for Mason.

"I'll leave you to it." Samuel nodded to Ericka and Charlotte, quitting Arlie's office with urgent, long-legged strides.

Arlie's imagination had always been vivid and vast, but this time, its services weren't required. She had breathed the very air from his lungs. Had felt him. Tasted him. Could taste him still.

And she wanted to taste him again.

She'd fought this knowledge all night and all morning. All her life, it seemed. Fought it while her senses fed on his proximity, a longing echoing through her whole being.

Last night had been like a single swallow of water after years of thirst.

It had only served to wake up the pure, sweet need. An ache that danced through the deepest parts of her.

She had wanted Samuel Kane then.

She wanted him now.

Wresting her attention from the man who had become her world's axis in the past twenty-four hours, she turned to Ericka and Charlotte. "Shall we?"

# Seven

Samuel Kane didn't like mistakes.

Mistakes were costly.

Last night had been one of them.

As it had every morning since he was eight, the grinding, relentless engine of his mind had woken him at promptly 4:00 a.m. with a blast of inexplicable dread. He lay there in the predawn dark, helpless to stop the careful, detailed rendering of his every misstep committed the previous day. A helpful catalog of evidence detailing what he had always known to be true.

No matter how hard he tried, how fast he ran, failure haunted his heels like a shadow.

This morning had been no different.

Until.

Until his mind reached the moment where he'd held

Arlie Banks in his arms and they'd kissed. She'd been so sweet. So eager.

It was every kind of wrong and destructive to *his plan*, but God, she'd felt so good.

Every cell in his body had demanded that he lift her off her heels, anchor her legs around his waist, and take her on the nearest horizontal surface. That's certainly what his brother would have done.

But he wasn't his brother.

He was his own, neurotic, complicated, cerebral self. So he had apologized for something that apparently required no apology.

Because it hadn't meant anything to her.

Logically, he understood this was the best possible outcome given the wrench he'd thrown into his plans.

His body didn't respond to logic.

It responded to *her*.

Try as he might, he couldn't erase the feeling of her from his skin.

He could have made a call that evening when he'd arrived home. He had a dependable list of numbers for women willing to relieve whatever needs he might have and leave his life blissfully uncomplicated.

Arlie Banks was complication personified.

Clearly, more careful orchestrations for Arlie and Mason's next encounter would be required. As it happened, the perfect opportunity arrived on his pristinely organized desk later that morning.

The marketing director for Willow Creek Winery, another of his father's less than wildly successful pet projects, requested assistance from the corporate office in launching a new ad campaign after they'd been fired by the branding agency they'd engaged.

Again.

Located across the country in Napa's Oak Knoll District, Willow Creek Winery had been a subject of contention since its purchase. A tangled history of fiscal mismanagement and poor planning, the winery had proved to be an epic pain in Samuel's ass since the papers had been signed.

Luckily, the vineyards were a mere ninety-minute limousine ride away from San Francisco, where Supply Side West would be launching the very next week.

Surely a long weekend in Napa with *the* Paul Martine, food photographer to the stars, would be enough to lure Arlie into volunteering assistance prior to the show. Especially when Samuel had communicated to him *precisely* what he had been hoping to capture with this particular photo shoot.

Mason was, as always, the wild card.

Samuel was reasonably sure he could get his brother there physically. Willow Creek had been one of Mason's favorite haunts since its purchase. A weekend alone with Arlie should add much needed incentive. But Samuel needed more than that.

He needed insurance.

And knew just how to get it.

Taking a deep, preparatory breath, Samuel stalked across the plush carpeting of his office and out into the hall, passing Charlotte's desk on the way.

She nodded to him in their customary nonverbal greeting, the monitor's glow making blue rectangles of her glasses as she squinted at an expense report.

"Nice job on the reception last night," he said, pausing at the corner of her desk. Knowing firsthand that his father was stingy with compliments, Samuel made a regular habit of offering them up to Charlotte whenever he could.

Charlotte's hunched shoulders lowered from her ears a fraction. "Thank you so much. I wasn't overly impressed with the caterer, but—"

"You did great. Don't let anyone tell you otherwise." He had regularly seen how her face fell when their father railed about a missed detail or lack of excellence in execution.

He knew the feeling.

"Is he free?" Samuel asked, nodding toward Mason's office.

"Until one," Charlotte answered, not even glancing at her monitor.

"Thanks."

Knocking brusquely on Mason's closed door, Samuel entered before being granted permission.

Like his own office, Mason's contained a collection of art and antiques the Philadelphia Museum of Art often asked to borrow. *Unlike* his, this precious collection was littered with discarded bagel wrappers, hastily scrawled notes, stacks of paper and scattered paperclips.

"Well, if it isn't my big brother." Mason took a sip from his Dartmouth Class of 2017 mug and set it down directly on the desk's mahogany surface, *not* on the coaster each executive had been provided. Behind him, the floor-to-ceiling windows presented a panorama of Philadelphia's Bond Street skyscrapers in the late-morning sunlight. A flock of birds sailed past, peppering the sky with coordinated movements that never failed to mesmerize him.

Samuel had rehearsed the next few words carefully

in the privacy of his own office, but experienced strange difficulty saying them now.

Moving aside the suit jacket sprawled across the chairs opposite Mason's desk like a discarded husk, Samuel seated himself. "I need—" he paused, his mouth suddenly filled with sand "—a favor."

Mason's grin might as well have revealed a bunch of yellow canary feathers as he leaned back in his chair, kicking his shoes to rest among the clutter. "You, asking for a favor? Is this one of the signs of the apocalypse?"

Clearing his gravelly throat, Samuel sat forward, thumbing the perfect pleat in his trousers. "You know Willow Creek has been struggling."

"Maybe not Dad's best acquisition." Mason twirled a pen in his fingers.

Samuel did his level best not to grind his teeth. "I'm thinking of assigning the styling shoot to Arlie as a first project, but frankly, I'm a little concerned."

To Samuel's great surprise, a furrow appeared between his brother's eyebrows. "About?"

"She's not especially familiar with the brand. And beyond that, I met a former coworker of hers from *Gastronomie* last night, and while she didn't tell me anything concrete, I got the impression that there might have been some challenges around her departure."

"What kind of challenges?" Mason asked.

"Again, I didn't get any specific information. This is just my impression."

"Are we talking about that weird psychoanalytic thing you do where you watch someone's face and make large, sweeping decisions about their motivating factors and moral compass?"

Biting down on his irritation, Samuel forced a smile. "That's not how I would describe it, but yes."

"What exactly would you like me to do?" As usual, Mason proved nearly impossible to read. Sympathy would have been helpful. Or unabashed self-interest. A motive Samuel trusted even more.

"You know how important this project is." Samuel looked his twin directly in eyes the precise color of his own. "I need feet on the ground. I need someone I can trust."

"I see," Mason said. "And you've trusted me since—" he hesitated, appearing to consider "—since when?"

Samuel released a heavy sigh. So much for the brotherly solidarity angle.

"I know in the past I may have come off somewhat… rigid."

"Somewhat?" Mason snorted, rocking back in his chair. "I've met steel rebar more flexible than you."

"I respect your perception." Each word felt like a shard of broken glass. "Which is precisely why I would like us to try and work more closely together. I thought this project might be an opportunity to do that. Provided you're available this weekend to help get the ball rolling."

Mason swung his feet beneath the desk and sat up straight. "I've got it covered."

"You're sure?" Samuel pressed. "You don't have any plans?"

"Plans?" Mason's smile was maddeningly obtuse. "What sort of plans do you think I might have?"

The sort that involved Mason's face buried so deep between female thighs that answering emails between

5:00 p.m. on Friday to 8:00 a.m. on Monday would be a near impossibility.

"If you do, it's fine. I just need to know now so I can—"

"I won't let you down, big brother." Mason rose from his chair and browsed among the copious piles of paper on his desk, thumbing each stack like an oracle reading runes.

"Honestly, you can stop with the big brother thing anytime. Sixty-three minutes hardly qualifies me for that title."

"It does in my book," Mason said. "And in my planner too. Which, thanks, by the way." He held aloft the hand-sewn, leather-bound planner Samuel had ironically gifted to him on their shared birthday. Frankly, he'd expected him to have tossed it in the trash at his earliest convenience.

"You use it?" Samuel asked.

"All the time."

If he had been forced to guess, Samuel would suspect it was mostly the contacts section. "I'm glad to hear it."

He stood up, facing his brother.

At moments like this, the strangeness of being a twin hit him with full force. Mason was an exceedingly inaccurate mirror. Every cell in their bodies was once exactly identical. But how different they were and had always been. How different they would always be.

"I'd appreciate if you could let me know how it goes," Samuel said.

"Oh, believe me, I will."

Samuel paused briefly in the doorway. Imagining Mason when confronted with what he'd laid in store was one thing. Imagining Arlie if everything went according to his plans was entirely another.

He crossed the marble breezeway back toward his office, stopping at Charlotte's desk. "Think you can get me a flight to Napa this weekend?"

"Of course." Charlotte nodded enthusiastically. "Flying out Friday after your four o'clock steering committee meeting?"

"Yes," he said. "Returning Thursday evening. Main cabin," he said. "Not first class."

Her look of surprise was almost canine in its purity and confusion. "Not…first class?"

Samuel knew exactly how strange this request must be. All Kanes flew first class according to his father's decree. When not via private jet.

"Main cabin," he confirmed.

"Would you still like an aisle seat?"

"Please," he said. The thought of being trapped in a window seat made his collar feel several sizes too tight.

"You got it." With that, her focus shifted back to her monitor, her fingers flying over the keyboard.

"There's just one more thing," Samuel said.

"What's that?"

"There's going to be a couple more attendees on this trip, and I need to make sure they're seated together."

"Not a problem," Charlotte said, keys clacking as her eyes darted over her monitor.

"Mason," he said. "And the new hire—"

"Arlie Banks," she finished for him.

"I haven't discussed this with her yet, but I'll be pointing her in your direction once I do. We both know how easily distracted Mason can be. I thought, this way, they could talk concepts on the way over."

"That makes perfect sense." Charlotte's expression revealed little in the way of her actual thoughts. "We have plenty of upgrades available, so taking care of Miss Banks shouldn't be a problem."

"I knew I could count on you." Samuel knocked on the glossy wood surface of her desk before turning to his office.

"I'll send the confirmation shortly," Charlotte said.

She did. Along with a reservation at the Fairmont, his father's favorite hotel.

With those details entered into his calendar, Samuel began his email to Paul Martine.

I can't thank you enough for being willing to take on this project at the last minute. I can't stress to you how specific my father's vision is for this shoot. No matter what, the following shots must, MUST be captured.

Typing out the details with vivid clarity, Samuel experienced a strange sensation.

He was smiling.

# Eight

Arlie totally hated this.

All this luxury. All this opulence.

Or so she tried to convince herself while enveloped in what she could only assume were twenty thousand count Egyptian cotton sheets that felt like melted butter on her freshly shaved legs.

It had begun the evening before with the first-class flight arranged by Charlotte Westbrook. Despite an apologetic text from Mason that he'd have to catch a later flight, a suited and booted chauffer bearing a miniature whiteboard with KANE neatly printed on it had been there to collect her. The final coup had been the butler who'd met her at the Kanes' personal quarters at Willow Creek Winery and escorted her to a room overlooking the sloped terraces of vineyards carved into the sprawling green hillside. It had a four-poster bed. A not-so-mini bar stocked with full-size bottles. A soaking tub the size of a small swimming pool.

Yep.

Definitely hated this.

She told herself that she missed the familiar comfort of her shoebox of an apartment overlooking an ally and a frequently overflowing dumpster. The patch of ceiling in the bathroom that was always mysteriously damp. The iron maiden of a closet.

As she had when she'd been little more than a girl wandering openmouthed through Fair Weather Hall, Arlie felt a familiar stab of wonder that this was how the Kanes lived every day.

Just as she had when her mother had begun working as their chef.

Their home had been nice enough. A neat suburban ranch that more than accommodated her, her mother and her father.

It had been reality. Screen door, backyard, seasonally decorated porch and all. The warm, happy place her family had returned to at the end of each day.

Happy, at least, where Arlie and her mother were concerned. An entirely different story had unraveled when her father came home from his long hours at the Midvale Steel plant.

It always started out okay.

Her mother cooking dinner for them long after the Kanes had already eaten, been bathed and tucked into bed.

A homey table spread for the three of them.

But as the night wore on and her father downed more and more beer, the conversation inevitably shifted to how what they were eating for dinner surely didn't measure up to whatever her mother had fixed for "those goddamned Kanes."

Arlie's mother always did her best to diffuse his bitterness, assuring her father that she both disliked the Kanes and that her real life was here, with them.

As much as it pained her to say, Arlie had doubted this a time or two.

Because she herself had been to the Kanes' estate and couldn't imagine any reality where her mother would prefer the small suburban house ruled over by her father's tempestuous moods.

And here she was as an adult, having the same conflicted thoughts. This only further served to foster a theory Arlie had held throughout the duration of her adult life. Home wasn't a place. Home was a state of being. The place you grew up in also grew up in you, whether you were Arlie Banks or Samuel Kane.

Speaking of the Kanes, Arlie was set to meet Mason in the kitchen in exactly ninety minutes. With a sigh of regret, she peeled herself out of the downy layers of bedding and padded barefoot into the bathroom, turning on the multi-headed marble shower while longingly eyeing the bathtub.

If she made it through this day without a potentially career-ending mishap, she promised herself an hourlong soak with the lavender bath salts in the basket full of goodies perched on the side of the tub.

After a quick shower, she slid into the fluffy bathrobe hung on the gilded hook outside the shower door and seated herself at the vanity.

For no reason she could say, she spent a little extra time smoothing on her foundation and powder, sweeping on eye shadow, and lining her eyes with the taupe eyeliner that conjured the sable rings around her irises. She stopped when it came time to apply lipstick.

Brushing the tips of her fingers over her lips, she surrendered to a feeling of awe. Samuel's mouth had been in the places she now touched. His tongue had stroked along the seam she now traced with the blade of her finger.

And *how* he had kissed her.

The control that governed every aspect of his life dissolving as something wild rose to the surface, threatening to drag her down, down into the inferno of unexpressed passion burning beneath his mannered calm.

Something in her had longed to answer that part of him. To meet it and stoke the flame until it engulfed them both. Consequences be damned.

Blowing out a frustrated breath, she selected a nude matte lipstick and slicked it over her lips.

To wardrobe.

On any normal shoot, she would have showed up in her favorite jeans, sneakers and a tank top. But something about Willow Creek inclined her toward polish.

She selected a simple black sleeveless shantung sheath. Formfitting, but not overtly attention-seeking. Sweeping her hair into a long, loosely romantic braid to keep it out of the way, she paused to examine herself in the full-length mirror.

She would do.

The screen on her phone lit up. She bent down to remove it from the charger and her stomach flipped when she saw the name on the screen.

Taegan.

Thumbing open the locked screen, she read the text.

Anything for me yet?

Knowing that her iPhone would send Taegan a read receipt, Arlie typed out an equally brief reply.

Working on it.

And she had been.

She had, in her bag, a file she'd managed to pilfer from Charlotte's desk and make copies of while she had been taking notes in a late meeting. It felt like the proverbial albatross, a heavy, rude thing slung around her neck, dragging her toward the earth.

Every time she glanced down at her bag, the same question immediately returned to her.

*Was she really capable of doing this?*

She hadn't yet been able to answer that question for herself.

Taegan's reply came swiftly.

See you soon. Enjoy Willow Creek.

Arlie's scalp prickled as a fizz of adrenaline further sped up her erratic heart. Taegan not only knew Arlie would be at Supply Side West, she knew she'd come early to visit the vineyards.

As she stood in the well-appointed foyer of a room she had no real right to occupy, a very unattractive idea unfolded in Arlie's mind.

Perhaps she wasn't the only employee of Kane Foods Taegan Lynch had been grooming to her service.

Glancing down at her phone again, Arlie saw that she only had four minutes to make her way to the chef's kitchen the concierge had pointed out during the tour last night.

Tucking the zip bag containing her tools of the trade under her arm, she deposited the brass room key and her cell phone into her pocket before sprinting off to meet Mason in the kitchen.

She got as far as the main hall when, rounding the corner, she collided with Parker Kane.

He made an exasperated sound, stepping back and dusting his ghost-gray suit jacket like he'd just been accosted by a soot-soiled street urchin. "Why don't you watch where you're going?" he thundered.

"I'm sorry," she said, attempting to conjure a brightness and enthusiasm that seeing him had sucked out of her. "I'm afraid I was just in a bit of a hurry."

Arlie forced herself to look him in the eye, remembering how she'd once been afraid Parker Kane's gaze would turn her to stone.

Perhaps she hadn't been entirely wrong.

His cold blue eyes bore into her, freezing her to the spot.

"I knew you had been invited to participate in the events, but I wasn't aware you would be staying at the *family* quarters." His features reflected the revulsion of a man addressing a cockroach.

Aware that an uncomfortable amount of time had passed, Arlie opened her mouth, horrified at the pathetic jumble of words tumbling past her lips like a bag of dropped apples.

"I… Mason said since we'd be doing the photo shoot here—"

"Photo shoot?" One silvery eyebrow rose. "I didn't authorize a photo shoot."

A fine sweat bloomed on her forehead, a single cold bead of moisture crawling down her ribs. She wasn't just a deer in the headlights. She swallowed the stone in her throat, attempting to square her shoulders.

"Samuel said—"

"Of course." Parker Kane's jaw hardened, his lips forming a flat, disapproving line. "Samuel seems determined to undermine my authority on all matters. He failed to ask for authorization for the photo shoot just as he failed to ask for authorization in hiring you. Had I been offered my rightful opportunity, I would have declined on both counts."

Arlie's heart fell from her chest and landed in her guts with a sickening splat. At the same time, a small blue flame of rage flickered at the base of her skull, fanned by years of simmering resentment. "Why is that?"

The Kane patriarch waited as a white-jacketed staff member pushed a tray of sliver-domed dishes past. "Your reputation precedes you, Miss Banks."

For one terrifying moment, Arlie considered the possibility that, with his considerable knowledge and influence, Parker Kane had somehow learned of the circumstances of her departure from *Gastronomie*.

"I'm not sure what you mean." A rusty fishhook cast into the ocean of her doubt.

"I'm sure you don't." He inclined his head, the ambient lighting overhead glinting off the frames of his designer glasses. "It suffices to say, like mother, like daughter."

Arlie didn't know what bothered her more. That he had the nerve to say this to her directly, or that he was as right about her as he had been wrong about her mother.

Yet even in the wake of her outrage, a warm tide of relief eased her shoulders away from her ears.

He didn't know the half of it.

"As pleasant as this conversation has been," Arlie said, glancing at her phone, "I'm late for the unauthorized photo shoot. If you'll excuse me." She pushed past him, doing her best to mimic the give-no-shits hauteur she'd frequently seen her best friend employ.

Legs shaking, she walked across the main hall with its cathedral ceiling and plush Persian carpets, ducking down the hallway bedecked with Dutch Masters with their gilded milkmaids and luridly sexy still lifes of delicate tulips and glossy tumbling fruit.

Had she known exactly what would be waiting for her in the kitchen, she might have paused for a moment to practice some deep breathing.

Paul Martine, the photographer whose images she had worshipped since she was old enough to reach the lifestyle rack in her local bookstore, stood squinting behind a camera anchored on a tripod.

He uttered a directive in rapid French to the black-clad assistant hovering by his elbow. She hurried off just as Paul peeked over the camera, noting Arlie's arrival.

"You are the food stylist?"

Arlie nodded, her mouth suddenly dry. "Yes," she said, shifting the strap of her tool case on her shoulder. "I'm Arlie Banks."

She held out her clammy hand, wishing like hell she'd paused outside the room to swipe it on her dress before entering the kitchen.

Paul shook it briskly, decisively, as his eyes the color of aged tobacco scanned the kitchen.

"But where is Mason Kane? I was told he was to be directing this shoot, *oui*?"

*"Oui,"* Arlie echoed. "That was my understanding as well."

As quickly as she was able, Arlie reviewed the details of their preproduction call. They were to shoot Willow Creek winery's cabernet, chardonnay and relatively new claret. Ericka had signed off on food being present as an offset. The winery's manager had been tasked with finding bottles with perfect labels and had agreed to source the appropriate glasses. Before boarding her plane, Arlie had put in calls to several artisan bakeries and a *fromagerie* all too eager to supply photogenic wedges of Gorgonzola and Brie for a shoot that had anything to do with the Kanes.

Mason had overseen all of this.

And now, no Mason.

Arlie dug her phone out of her pocket and checked to see if she'd received any messages.

She had.

A brief but very apologetic email from Mason.

Pressing business. Urgent priorities. Forgiveness requested.

"I'm afraid that Mason won't be joining us," Arlie said, part of her still not quite comprehending that she was actually talking to *the* Paul Martine.

*"Merde!"* Paul dug his hands into his thick crop of salt-and-pepper hair, and it somehow fell right back into place. He paced the length of the kitchen, the clack of his black ostrich-skin cowboy boots echoing in the cavernous space.

Having exactly one semester of college French, Arlie could make out the words *light* and *tomorrow* and *cloudy* hidden like Easter eggs among a florid cascade of elegant curses.

"Would you give me just a moment?" she asked.

Martine waved her away like he might a mosquito.

Pulling up the contacts on her cell phone, Arlie looked down at the name, and taking a deep breath, pressed the call button.

He answered after 1.5 rings.

"Samuel Kane," he said.

As if he didn't have her number saved in his phone.

As if he hadn't wrapped his fingers around the back of her head and angled her neck so he could pillage her mouth less than forty-eight hours before.

"Hi. This is Arlie."

Silence spiraled out between them.

"I'm terribly sorry to bother you. It's just…I'm here with the photographer and I got an email from Mason and it seems he's going to be unable to make it."

"*Fuck!* I'll be right there."

The line went dead.

She told herself it was nervousness, not excitement, that had set a sudden swarm of butterflies loose in her middle.

Martine's assistant returned with a hesitantly penitent smile and a steaming demitasse of espresso, which Paul took without looking.

"Mason's brother, Samuel, is coming." To Arlie, it sounded like an apology she wasn't certain she owed. In her past life, neither the chief marketing officer nor the chief executive officer would have had anything to do with the photo shoot itself after their directives had been doled out. But then, the Kanes, or at least Samuel, seemed to have a far more hands-on relationship with the daily operations of their empire. His instructions had been as direct as they were odd. The photo shoot absolutely, positively, was not to start without Mason present.

She set her bag on the marble counter and began to unpack her tools.

Nitrile gloves to handle the glasses. A spray bottle. Glycerin to mix with water to create the effect of condensation for chilled white wine. A travel bottle of dish soap, should the red wine need assistance with the bubbles that often appeared when freshly poured. Wooden skewers, should the bubbles require encouragement to form attractive gatherings. Sheets of muslin, and white and black foam core boards for taming and sculpting the natural light that Ericka had been absolutely insistent upon in their preproduction meeting.

Arlie couldn't ask for better windows.

Or a better room, for that matter.

The pure, gilded light of the rising sun poured in from floor-to-ceiling panes overlooking the stepped rows of meticulously attended vines.

On the other side of the kitchen, Arlie recognized the gleaming expanse of the black-lacquered, chrome-handled La Cornue Château Supreme oven. Half of her wanted to forget the shoot altogether and prostrate herself in front of it.

Samuel arrived a mere five minutes later, looking impossibly handsome and exceedingly irritated.

She wasn't sure if it was the fact that he was on family turf or that she'd caught him on the fly, but Samuel had forgone his customary coat, wearing instead a crisp, deep blue shirt the color of the summer sky before a storm. The sleeves were rolled up to the elbow, revealing the sloping lengths of muscle on his forearms. Jeans were too much to hope for, Arlie knew, but the European-cut dark gray slacks he wore revealed the powerful topography of his legs just as well.

The temperature in the room seemed to rise by a few degrees when Samuel's eyes found hers. It could have been her imagination, or wishful thinking, but she could have sworn his lips softened ever so slightly, the barest crinkle teasing the corners of his eyes.

Then as quickly as they had landed on her, they moved to Martine. Samuel almost looked relieved to have a direction to walk in that didn't involve Arlie.

"Samuel Kane," he said, holding out his hand.

Martine shook his hand briefly before dropping it with a sound of disgust.

"I come all the way from Paris on a red-eye flight and nothing is ready. *Nothing!*"

A hot flush crept into Arlie's cheeks. Being made to look inept in front of Samuel was right up there with recreational flaying on her list of Fun Things to Do. "I'm not sure I understand," she said. "The bottles are right there. And the food pairings we discussed—"

"Are useless without the models."

Arlie blinked, aware that her face must have had an almost comical look of confusion. "Models? There were no models discussed in preproduction."

Martine motioned to his assistant, who handed over a folded sheaf of papers. "It is right here. I received an email with the details." He slapped it down on the marble counter.

Arlie reached for it, but Samuel got there first. He

unfolded the papers and read, his expression inscrutable. With a grunt of disgust, he balled up the papers in his fist and shot them into the trash. "You're just going to have to change your plans, Mr. Martine."

Arlie elbowed Samuel, widening her eyes in an *Are you out of your mind?* look.

Famously temperamental, Paul Martine had been known to walk off set if the sparkling water on his extensive rider wasn't the right temperature.

This was her first official project, and she badly needed this win.

"I think what Samuel was trying to say," Arlie said, reaching for the paper bag containing bread from the local bakery, "is maybe we could just focus on the wine itself? I have some lovely rosemary focaccia here and I could make a charcuterie board. Those are trending on Instagram."

Martine wasn't listening to her.

His assistant had leaned in, whispering something in his ear that made his bushy eyebrows rise in surprise. They stepped back, both of them looking at her and Samuel not unlike prize truffles at the Alba World Auction.

"Yes," Martine said decisively. "Yes, you will do. Powder." He snapped his fingers and the assistant scurried off.

"I'm sorry," Arlie said. "I'm not sure I understand."

Martine ducked behind the tripod, swinging the lens in their direction before pressing the shutter release. Glancing down at the preview screen, he nodded brusquely. "Handsome husband, beautiful wife. Yes. *Ça marche.*"

"Oh," Arlie said, realization finally crystallizing in her mind. "Oh, no. We're not—"

"Out of the question," Samuel echoed, sounding even more alarmed than Arlie. "Absolutely not."

"Cecile," Martine called. "We pack the equipment."

"Wait!" Arlie shot Samuel a pleading look, hoping to telegraph exactly how much this chance meant to her.

Samuel sighed, his broad shoulders sinking with his exhale. "These are only to be used for international advertising campaigns, you understand? Foreign markets *only*."

"Of course," Arlie agreed hastily, exhilaration sparkling through her like champagne bubbles As she launched into action. In fifteen minutes, she'd set the scene. A table on the balcony outside the kitchen. Chardonnay for her, cabernet for him, a dropper full of distilled water helping to banish the inkiness and tease out the deep garnet tones. Between them, a rustic cutting board with architecturally arranged cheeses, a tumble of fat, glistening figs.

Arlie leaned in, adjusting one of the stems with a pair of tweezers.

"Enough," Martine snapped. "We lose the light."

Samuel sat with a Kleenex tucked into the collar of his shirt, Cecile patting his forehead with a blotting sponge.

Arlie had to bite the inside of her cheek to keep from smiling. She couldn't remember if she'd ever seen a man look more miserable.

"Behind the table. Go." Martine pointed toward the bistro table overlooking the sloping fields of the vineyard.

Cecile liberated the Kleenex and ushered them over, posing them like oversized dolls.

And there they were.

Face to face. Samuel's arm around Arlie's waist, his mouth hovering a mere five inches away, sunlight slanting through their glasses, held mid-toast.

Fighting to keep breath in her lungs, Arlie compelled herself to meet his gaze. "I think she missed a spot," she said, hoping to puncture the tension thickening the air between them.

Samuel didn't respond, didn't smile. His breathing quickened, feathering her cheeks.

Dizzied by his nearness, the scent of his skin, Arlie anchored her fingers in the fabric of his shirt.

"Closer," Martine demanded. "You are in love. You cannot wait to kiss her."

Samuel dropped his head until she could feel the warmth of his lips mere centimeters away from hers. Her belly felt heavy, her heart pumping blood to the deepest parts of her as a sympathetic ache woke between her thighs.

God, she wanted this man. Wanted to feel his weight on her.

In her.

*"Oui, oui, oui!"* Martine snapped erratically. *"Donne-moi plus!"*

*Give me more.*

*Oh, yes, please, God. Give me more. Give me everything.*

Give me *you.*

Reckless, breathless, Arlie lifted her chin so her lips grazed Samuel's. That first delirious taste of him. Coffee-laced, intoxicating.

Samuel pulled back abruptly. The startled look in his eyes mirrored her own shock.

The photo shoot. The photographer. The assistant. What was she doing?

She didn't know. And for the first time, she didn't care. She just needed to be nearer to him. And if pretending to be a happy couple was the vehicle, she would drive it. All these months of fear and scarcity. Of doubt and despair. She wanted this one good thing. Selfishly and without apology.

His lips skimmed over hers in answer. Hesitant. A question.

*This?*

*Us?*

Then Parker Kane's image rose up in Arlie's memory, his look accusatory and knowing. Those cold blue eyes reducing her to the one fact she couldn't outrun.

*He wouldn't want you if he knew.*

A surge of nausea rocked her on unsteady feet. Feeling like she'd been punched in the stomach, Arlie backed away, leaving Samuel staring at her in confusion.

"I'm sorry," she said. "I'm so sorry. I need to go."

Arlie grabbed her bag, shoving her tools into it before darting into the hallway, her phone and the incriminating message on it burning her like a hot coal.

# Nine

When Samuel stepped into the formal dining room of the Kane family's private residence at Willow Creek, his father was waiting for him.

Because of course he was.

Perched at the head of the fifteen-foot-long antique dining room table with the SUV-sized fireplace crackling behind him, Parker Kane resembled an exceptionally well-dressed Satan. His posture was the same as it always was at their formal family dinners: back straight, shoulders squared, forearms—but not elbows— extended on the table before him. His hands, palms down as if he, and not gravity, held the table to the earth.

"Samuel."

If life had taught him anything, there were plenty of nicknames that could be derived from his name. But damned if his father had ever used a single one. Samuel had been to friends' houses as a boy on "play dates" foisted on him by his mother, and often wondered at how freely and casually affection was expressed between fathers and their sons. An arm draped around the shoulders. Hair ruffled into absurd feathers by a warm paternal hand.

Witnessing it had always made Samuel's heart feel like a small cold stone in his chest.

Not that his mother hadn't tried to make up for what his father lacked. Often as not, Samuel would duck from under her hand like a cat, glancing in his father's direction to make sure he'd seen that he didn't require cuddling and coddling.

"Father."

Parker Kane gestured to the chair he expected to Samuel to take. For the first time in his life, and for reasons he could not say, Samuel walked to the opposite side of the table and parked himself halfway down.

A lifelong expert in anticipating his father's displeasure, Samuel instantly registered the ponderous crease appearing between his eyebrows, once an inky black but now threaded with silver. Beneath them, his blue eyes hardened from lake water to iceberg.

"Is there a particular reason you chose not to join us on the jet?" The polished-marble sound of his father's voice sent a chill rolling down Samuel's spine. As he had since he was eighteen, he had to remind himself he was no longer afraid.

"I had a video call with the Campbell team." Samuel leaned back in his chair. "Are you equally distressed about Mason failing to show up yet again?"

"No." His father signaled to the perfectly starched

attendant, who darted to his side like an eager hummingbird. "Aisla T'Orten 105, neat."

The MBA in Samuel couldn't help but calculate what two ounces from a $1.4 million dollar bottle of 105-year-old scotch would cost.

Roughly, a hundred grand would soon be disappearing down his father's gullet.

"For you, sir?"

"Nothing," Samuel said with a stab of savage satisfaction. Few things angered his father like the willful rejection of the luxury he so benevolently doled out. Which was precisely why Samuel had made a lifelong habit of turning away advantages afforded him. From working a summer job at a car wash to covering the tuition of a university not approved by the Kane patriarch to wearing off-the-rack suits and shirts.

The dining room attendant bustled off, leaving them in an awkward silence broken only by the crackling fire.

"Mason will be flying up tomorrow," his father said. "He had pressing business to attend to."

*Right*, Samuel thought. *Like pressing his dick into some bored, married socialite.* "Again?" he asked, startled by the sudden sound of his own voice in the cavernous dining hall.

"What did you just say?" Thunderheads gathered in his father's voice.

"I said, *again*?" Blood thundered in Samuel's ears as adrenaline surged in in his veins. What in God's name was he *doing*?

"I don't believe I take your meaning," his father said, calmly lacing his long fingers together and resting them on the table before him.

Samuel had learned early and often that the more

polite his father's diction became, the more likely the conversation was to end in scorched earth, crushed egos, and occasionally, tears. His own, in his childhood. These days it was primarily members of the board of directors, and the occasional sales executive, whom Parker Kane reduced to quivering-lipped, brimming-eyed apologies.

And sometimes a mea culpa wine-and-cheese basket.

This was the time to back down. To back up. To move in any other direction than the trouble his mouth seemed determined to catapult him into.

With growing dread, Samuel realized he had no intention of stopping. "Don't you ever get tired of making excuses for him? Of trying to make it seem like he actually gives a damn about Kane Foods?"

At that precise moment, the attendant returned to the table, scotch gleaming like petrified amber in the Baccarat cut crystal tumbler, "Here you are, Mr. Kane."

"Thank you," his father said in the surgically precise tone he reserved for anyone in a service position. He lifted the glass, letting the firelight play with the crystal's refractive angles. "Mason is a maverick. A risk taker. He doesn't use numbers or rules or schedules as a crutch. I don't expect you to understand."

"No," Samuel said, relishing the shock on his father's face. "It's you who don't understand. But you will."

"Oh, good," Marlowe said, breezing into the dining room with her obsequious Yalie fiancé in her wake. "You haven't started yet."

In a cloud of good perfume and bad cigars, they assumed their appointed places at the table opposite Samuel. Their father stood, planting a dry kiss on his sister's cheek before clapping Neil affectionately on the back.

Samuel watched as Neil allowed his sister to pull out her own chair before he took his own. After they were seated, he flopped a possessive, Versace suit-coat-clad arm around her elegant bare shoulders. Samuel suffered a sympathetic shudder of revulsion as Neil's waxy, tapered fingertips lazily trailed up Marlowe's neck.

The attendant reappeared, taking Marlowe's order of Willow Creek house cabernet and Neil's request of whatever it was their father was drinking as he "trusted his taste."

Obsequious little prick.

Their father cleared his throat and looked at each of his children in turn. "Now that you're both here, there's a matter I would like to discuss with you."

Samuel and Marlowe straightened up in tandem, all too familiar with the carnage that often followed that line of dialogue.

"It has come to my attention that a new hire was made recently. One that I was neither apprised of or approved." His father took another sip of his scotch. "Arlington Banks."

Samuel's teeth clenched. "It was my understanding that you were to be consulted on VP-level positions and above. Arlie—Arlington Banks is a senior food stylist."

"This is precisely the kind of thing I mean." His father leaned forward, skewering Samuel with his gaze. "You obey the letter of the law, but don't think twice about hiring her when you know the kind of family she comes from."

Samuel drew a long, steadying breath to combat the pure limbic rage crackling along his nerves. "And what does that mean?"

"After the regrettable incident with her mother, how

can you possibly think of bringing her into this organization without consulting me first?"

*Regrettable incident.*

A rather sanitized way of describing the events leading to Arlie's mother being accused of stealing and her father showing up drunk and enraged once she'd been fired.

"Children shouldn't be judged by the sins of their parents," Samuel said. The irony of this statement was not lost on him. He had learned at his father's knee how to exploit small businesses, promising them aid while slowly draining their profits.

And then there was Millhaven Foods, which he tried never to think about.

"Corrupted roots produce corrupted fruit." His father adjusted the salad fork in his place setting so it was the precisely mandated half inch from its neighbor. "As I informed Miss Banks this morning."

Samuel saw red. The back of his high-backed chair made abrupt contact with the marble floor and sent a resounding crack rolling through the dining room as he stood. "You did what?"

Swirling the glass of tawny liquid, his father didn't even bother to look him in the eye. "I ran into Miss Banks quite unexpectedly and felt it incumbent on me to share my thoughts. As I am well within my rights to do in my own home."

"How dare you?" This question had circled in Samuel's thoughts from the time he had been ten years old.

Then, it had been summoned when his father had insisted that his mother, happy and beautiful in a knee-length, emerald-green dress, change before a benefit, informing her that she didn't make the "correct impression."

But this was the first time he'd actually spoken the words out loud to the man.

"Perhaps you should take an evening constitutional to recover your composure. You seem quite out of sorts, Samuel."

Across the table, Marlowe sent him a wide-eyed *don't do this look*.

It was already done.

Or he was. He had been for a long time.

"Arlie Banks is a talented, passionate professional, and will be an asset to Kane Foods International. You're just too blinded by a ridiculous grudge to see it."

An ugly smile folded his father's papery cheeks. "I suspect *I'm* not the one who's blinded when it comes to this particular topic."

Samuel's fists tightened, his mind seething with all the things he wanted to say.

"You may serve," his father said, motioning to the table with all the ceremony of an orchestral conductor.

Only then did he notice the white-coated team bearing silver-domed dishes, nervously hovering in the doorway from the kitchen. On cue, the staff descended, simultaneously placing the dishes in front of each of them before removing the lids with a flourish.

"Do sit down, Samuel." Unfolding the pristine white napkin, his father laid it across his lap with practiced ease.

"I'm not hungry," he announced. This too was a lie. Samuel was ravenous. But not for food.

He needed to see Arlie.

Now.

# Ten

Arlie stood in the shower's scalding spray, letting the water beat down on her shoulders. While it leached a measure of the tension from her body, it couldn't wash away Samuel Kane. Even now, the feeling of him lived just under her skin, easily summoned to the surface with a single errant thought.

She had been stupid today. So, incredibly, stupid.

Martine had captured at least a few usable pictures, she was sure of it. But she'd never walked out on a shoot.

*Walked?* Let's be honest. She had *run*. Fled all the way to her room where she had stayed, periodically checking her cell phone in expectation of a *What the actual fuck is wrong with you?* call/text from Samuel.

It never came.

If only she'd been so lucky where Taegan was concerned. Even now she could see the words of her message crawl across the backs of her eyelids like so many spiders as she dug her hands into her wet, soapy hair.

Tomorrow, 9:00 pm. Coyote Bar. Private room. Highly recommend you bring materials for discussion.

Once upon a time, Arlie had been ordinary. Boring.

A person with good credit and a nice apartment overlooking Fairmount Park. A person with regular dentist checkups. A clean driving record. Nothing to hide. No one to fear.

Thinking back to the precise moment when her life had run off the rails, she forced herself to confront a particularly uncomfortable question.

Had she known?

Had she known, when she'd accepted Hugh Morris's invite for a private dinner, how this would ultimately end up?

How, over oysters three ways, in trying to solve her immediate problems, she'd create much longer lasting ones?

Inadvertent disclosure.

Such a banal sounding term for a mistake with the power to dismantle her life as she'd known it. One conversation about her researching food styling trends on social media for a new project at *Gastronomie*, and a chain reaction of disaster had been set in motion. A sharp rap on her door startled her out of her misery. She'd propped it open with the door latch in the event that the room service she ordered arrived before she finished boiling herself alive.

"Just a minute!" she called, twisting off the shower. Opening the shower door, she dried herself off and slid into one of the complimentary plush robes, gathering the long skein of her hair and squeezing the water out of it with a towel before draping it over her shoulder.

Good enough for food delivery. She exited the bathroom in a cloud of steam and pulled open the propped door.

Samuel Kane appeared in the gap.

Only he didn't look like Samuel Kane.

He looked like wrath in a suit. Jaw set, muscles flexing, the mouth a thin, grim, line. Eyes blazing emerald above chiseled cheekbones. The cords on his neck rising like taut ropes.

"Oh," she said dumbly. "Hi."

A sinking feeling of self-consciousness further heated her already shower-warmed skin as he stared at her. His nostrils flared as he looked from her hair to her face, to the downy white bathrobe.

"Do you want to come in?" she added when he made no reply.

She stepped aside to grant him entry, catching the subtle scent of him as he moved past her into the entryway.

"Why didn't you tell me?" he asked.

Arlie's heart sank into her guts. There were too many answers to this question. And too many questions he didn't even know to ask.

"Tell you what?" she asked, opting for the safest path.

*Coward.*

Samuel stepped closer, her white robe reflected in his glacier-green eyes. "About my father. About what he said to you this morning."

The relief was so complete and acute it actually made

her dizzy. She pressed a palm against the wall to steady herself. All at once, the entryway seemed far too small to contain them.

"Our families have a lot of shared history," Arlie said. "Not all of it good."

"He had no right—"

"I'm sorry," she interrupted, knowing it was a weak and deliberate dodge. She didn't want to talk about this. Not with him. "It's absolutely mandatory that you surrender your tie and suit jacket for this conversation. I'm entirely underdressed and frankly feeling a little vulnerable about it."

Samuel walked into the well-appointed sitting area, shrugged off his suit jacket and laid it across the chaise longue. They snagged gazes as he gripped the knot of his tie, loosening it with small deliberate strokes. Finally, and with a tantalizing precision, he slid the tie from his neck, casting it off across his discarded jacket.

"Better?" he asked.

On a different night, in a different universe, it would have ended there.

But for reasons she could neither explain nor ignore, Arlie padded barefoot across the space between them.

"Almost." Lifting her hands to his neck, she undid the button closest to his collar. Then another. And another.

To her great surprise and delight, Samuel wore no T-shirt underneath.

She traced an idle finger over his Adam's apple.

He swallowed, the hard knot rising and falling beneath her touch.

Dizzy with desire, Arlie tilted her face up to his. The air was crackling and sizzling with electricity, with anticipation. The breathless inevitability of this thing between them making her feel loose-limbed and drunk. Invincible and terrified.

"All my life, I could have anything I wanted." Cupping her jaw, he ran the pad of his thumb over her lower lip. "Except you."

Arlie's breath came in irregular bursts, something deep inside her tightening at his admission. "You want me?"

Samuel only looked at her, but his silence said it all.

His wordlessness the purest part of what he had always given her.

The look that passed between them was both question and answer.

*Yes?*

*Yes.*

Arlie closed her lips over his thumb, drawing it into the wet warmth of her mouth.

His eyelids fell closed as a sound half pain and half prayer rumbled up from his chest.

She traced the tip of her tongue over the ridges of his fingerprint, imagining she could still taste book pages there.

He walked her backward, his weight pressing her against the wall as he withdrew his thumb from her mouth. The tips of his four fingers found the valley of naked skin between the snowdrifts of her robe, trailing along her neck, her chest, dipping beneath the fabric to find her nipple, already hard against the cloth. Slowly, lazily, he moved his thumb over it, making her gasp as he gently pinched it between his thumb and forefinger.

He'd done the same thing in the sacred darkness of a closet when they were eighteen.

He claimed her lips, tongues tangling in a devouring frenzy.

Arlie moaned into his mouth when he found the tie to her robe and loosed it. Cool air kissed her still-damp skin, the contrast delicious and illicit.

He broke their kiss and moved down her throat, lips scorching a trail over the sensitive flesh.

Flicking the robe open, he brought his mouth to her nipple. Sucking, nipping, grazing, until she was half mad. Her fingers tangled into the dark silky strands of his hair as his hand slid over her stomach and lower. Deliciously lower.

His grunt of approval vibrated through her chest as his fingers found the slick, aching place between her thighs. Teasing the sensitive bundle of nerves, he coated it with her own drenching desire.

Moving his mouth from her breast, he looked up at her, waiting until he had her undivided attention. "Do you want me to make you come?" These words pronounced in that voice. *His* voice. So measured. So controlled.

"Oh, God, yes. Please," she panted, her knees already weakening with the prospect.

Increasing the delicious friction, Samuel kept his thumb on her clit while he slipped his finger inside her. Filling her. Exploring her. Locating the spot that made the world around them go dusky and blue.

She fell forward, open, wet mouth on his naked shoulder.

"You like that?" he asked.

"Very much," she gasped, struggling for both oxygen and sanity.

His other hand found her hair, fingers threading into

a gentle grip that sent chills cascading down her neck. He angled her face toward his and Arlie knew instinctively it was so he could watch her. To read in her eyes the pleasure he had created.

Arlie bucked against his hand, years of want overriding all reason. Several selves aligned. Wanting him. Wanting this.

Samuel quickened his pace, matching her desperate undulations as she rode the groundswell at her center, threatening to wash her out to sea for now and forever.

His lips were hot at her ear, offering encouragement. Saying every single thing she had ever wanted to hear.

"I wanted you from the moment you first set foot in our house."

Arlie's hips backed against the cool wood of the closet door in rhythmic strokes.

"I wanted you as you stood there in your sundress trying not to look at me in the kitchen."

His fingers ventured deeper now, kindling a fire of a depth beyond her knowledge or experience. Her legs began to shake, her fingernails digging into his arms.

"I was only pretending to read, hoping you would come to the library to watch me. I would sit there staring at pages for hours and not remember a single word. Waiting for you."

She no longer had control of anything. Not her body. Not her life. Not her destiny.

Her core began to clench. All of her gathering around a single point that galloped toward a cliff into blackness.

*"Samuel."* It was urgent, this message. A white flag, a plea. She was undone. Under his complete care and command.

"Yes," he said, his voice glowing with the dangerous heat of a banked coal. "Come for me."

As if she had any choice.

Overcome by rippling pulses of pleasure like she had never known, she surrendered.

Undone. Lost in a firestorm of bliss. Every part of her both heavy and light as a new galaxy of stars unfolded behind the lids of her closed eyes.

Limp and boneless with the bliss he had given her, Arlie sagged against him.

"What do *you* want, Arlie Banks?" he asked.

But now, Arlie was the one with no words. No thoughts. She was pure sensation, existing only in the aftermath of Samuel Kane. Her breath sawing erratically in and out of her, she looked at him in the lamp's golden glow. The dark hair he usually kept so pin-neat hanging carelessly across his forehead. Eyes usually so focused and sharp now hazy with undisguised desire. His mouth, like hers, kiss swollen, glistening.

Chaos became him.

Arlie wanted to feed it. Some reckless depth inside her recognizing its own kind, a thing that lived in both of them, begging for liberation. Longing to surrender all control.

"Tell me," he urged.

Before this moment, she would have given him any number of answers.

*I want you to never stop looking at me the way that you're looking at me now.*

*But he will. Once he knows, he will.*

"You." With her eyes still on his, she reached out, palm flat against his rigid length beneath the tailored slacks. "I want you."

* * *

"Take me."

Samuel gazed down at Arlie, who had never looked more beautiful than she did in that moment. Lust-hazed eyes a deep sapphire blue, lips kiss-swollen rubies, cheeks flushed pink, her hair wild and the color of rain-soaked wheat fields.

She reached up and loosened his hand from her hair, maintaining eye contact as she took a step back from him. With one decisive movement, she shrugged the robe from her shoulders, standing before him naked and entire. No barriers. No artifice.

In the ensuing silence, he heard the sharp intake of his own breath as he drank her in. He allowed himself this moment to explore her hollows and curves like a shoreline to be charted, reining in the overwhelming desire to be inside her as quickly as he could lift her onto his throbbing cock.

From the minute she'd stepped into his office for her job interview, he'd sensed her hesitance. Her disbelief that she could have what she wanted. That what she wanted would be taken away.

He wanted her to take it back.

To take from him what she wanted.

With a sly, sexy smile unfolding on her lips, she took his hand, tugging him toward the end of the bed.

"Here," she said, strategically positioning them before the antique wood-framed cheval mirror.

Gently, reverently, she removed his shirt from his torso before running her hand from his bared sternum to his stomach, his muscles shivering under her touch. She paused at his navel, tracing a finger around the taut, small place where his life had begun.

His belt buckle clinked as she fumbled it open and reached beneath it to unbutton his pants, their eyes meeting as she slid the zipper down. Samuel's breath came faster now, heaving as she helped him step out of his pants, so that the only thing remaining between them was a pair of boxer briefs.

Arlie dipped her finger beneath the elastic rim, finding the pearly bead of moisture at the head of his cock and spreading it in concentric circles that made him suck air through his clenched teeth.

"I want to taste you." Her voice was breathy, a trace of uncertainty still lingering in her eyes.

"Then taste me."

Sinking to her knees, Arlie dragged the boxers down with her, freeing his erection.

He thought of their first, furtive kiss in the closet. With those same lips, she took him in her mouth, moving up and down his length.

"God, you're good at that," he breathed.

Her hands anchored themselves on his hipbones, pulling him toward her, quickening her pace then stopping altogether.

Samuel gazed down at her.

"Watch," she said, meeting his eyes in the mirror.

And he watched.

He watched as she flicked her tongue over his swollen head, her lips trailing down to the base of his cock before she took him in her mouth once again.

She brought her hand up, fastening around his length as she worked her mouth over him in a rhythm that echoed the throbbing of his heart.

His grip on her hair tightened, halting her progress. "Baby," he ground out, "I can't take much more."

Pulling against him, she deliberately took as much of him as she could.

A dare.

Samuel jerked back from her, lifting her to her feet before scooping her up and carrying her to the bed.

She lay as she had been deposited, ankles together. An invitation to be opened.

He joined her on the bed, drawing her knees apart as he hooked his forearms beneath her thighs, planting his hands on either side of her rib cage.

He found her mouth again, but this time, it was different. Her tongue tangling with his, their teeth grazing as a dark, sharp, hungry edge crept into their kiss. Each of them taking as much as possible, on this one impossible night.

Arlie tore away from their kiss, breathless, urgent. "Please," she said, looking up at him, skin glowing with a thin sheen of sweat.

"Please what?" he asked, needing to hear her say the words.

"Please fuck me."

Positioning himself at her opening, he kept his eyes locked on hers as he pushed into her with one long, slow, deliberate stroke.

A low groan escaped him as he sank into her, feeling her fire and silk as he came to rest against the deepest part of her. He lingered there for a moment, looking for confirmation that she wanted him to continue.

What he saw in her eyes instead nearly unmanned him right then and there.

Wonder.

"Arlie—" he began, losing his words again to a full body shudder.

"I know," she said, reaching up to push a sweat-kissed lock of hair away from his forehead. "I feel it too."

He began to move.

Slowly at first, the shifting muscles of his back tensing as he learned her. She gripped his buttocks with eager hands, tightening around him with every thrust, driving her hips up to meet him blow for blow.

"Let go," she whispered.

For the first time in Samuel's twenty-eight years, he did.

He surrendered. To whatever this was. To whatever consequences it brought. Sensation flooded in, blotting out the last of his tangled, complicated rules and thoughts. There was only her body and his. The fire between them.

He became aware of the desperate animal noises coming from her. Her nails clawing at his back.

Through his own pleasure-fogged gauge, he watched her climax roll over her features like storm clouds, knowing he was close the same way he knew lightning was coming in the seconds before it struck.

"Oh, God, Arlie."

The electric charge built at the base of his spine and pinwheeled outward until it was no longer confined to the low, deep, delicious ache behind his cock. It raced down his legs, spilled into his chest, his back, then ebbed into his heart.

A cry more primal than he had known himself capable of tore itself from Samuel's very soul as pleasure rocked through him in rhythmic waves. His body tensed as he collapsed to his elbows, burying his nose in the silky sweet tangle of her hair as he descended back toward earth.

They lay like that in absolute silence, his heart beating against hers through the thick wall of his chest as their breathing gradually slowed.

She gently ran her nails over his back. Up. Down. As if memorizing his topography.

He settled into her further, his body going slack, the ridge of his hips pressing against her inner thighs as he ceased all effort to hold himself up.

For the first time in as long as he could remember, Samuel wanted to break the silence. To make this moment real by the sound of his own voice. But making it real would mean dealing with the consequences of what they'd just done.

He wasn't ready for that.

Not yet.

Samuel eased off her, flopping onto his back. Above them, the blades of the fan made slow, lazy circles. They reminded him of a clock. Precious seconds ticking away.

Arlie rolled onto her side, her face half buried in the pillow, one sleepy eye fixed on him. She pushed a sweat-dampened clump of hair away from his forehead.

"What are you thinking?" she whispered.

"I'm thinking that I owe you an apology."

"For what?" she asked in a voice already thickening with sleep.

The dark fringe of her eyelashes raised, lowered, then dropped to her cheek.

"For everything," he whispered.

Her breath deepened and slowed, evening into the rhythm of sleep. Samuel joined her in the dark, letting the oblivion wipe the familiar sting of failure from his mind.

He had damned them both.

# Eleven

In the literature Samuel had studied growing up, sleeping women were frequently compared to angels.

Arlie Banks certainly looked like one, her hair spilling over the pillow like spun gold in the grayish predawn light. Her dark eyelashes feathered against a cheek bearing the ghosts of freckles from happier summers past, long, slim fingers resting on the pristine white of the sheet between them, her cuticles bitten raw.

But angels didn't struggle in their sleep the way Arlie did.

At four o'clock this morning, Samuel had woken up to her urgently moaning in her sleep. For a brief moment, he'd thought she might be reliving one of the livelier portions of their evening together.

Odd how passion and panic could sound so similar.

He had only watched at first, his eyes adjusting to the moonlight as he searched her face.

It didn't take long before he'd realized it wasn't passion playing on the hidden screen of her subconscious. Eyelids flickering, mouth drawn into a tight, terrified line.

Despite the overwhelming urge to reach out and place a soothing hand on her chest, Samuel held back, having remembered something his mother had told him once about night terrors, and how dangerous it could be to wake someone who suffered from them.

Small mewls of protest followed. Then her body had begun to twitch. Then her foot swept out, catching him in the shin as she uttered a distinct *Noooooo* as she wrestled with unseen demons.

Which was when he knew what he needed to do.

He'd been a complete and utter idiot, surrendering to his baser instincts the way that he had.

His plan to oust Mason had been compromised irreparably. Yet another misguided attempt on his part to have any level of control over his own destiny.

The one saving grace was that, as of yet, no one knew what had happened between them. If he could keep it that way, he might have a shot at saving Arlie a world of pain.

Drawing in one long, deep breath, he drank his last of Arlie Banks naked and serene.

He peeled back the sheets and scooted to the side of the bed, locating his boxer briefs. Next came his slacks, which he hastily stepped into, quickly fastening the belt.

"Hey, you."

Samuel spun to find Arlie sitting up in bed, sheets

clutched to her chest like a snowdrift, passion-mussed hair unspeakably alluring.

"Hi," he said. Lifting his shirt from the heap on the floor, he shrugged into it and began fastening the buttons.

"What's with the hurry?" she asked in a relaxed voice that didn't match her nocturnal turmoil at all. "The first Supply Side West event isn't until this evening. We have plenty of time to—"

"I have to go." Returning to the entryway to retrieve his tie from the chaise, Samuel slid it around his neck, all thumbs as he tried to execute the knot.

"Let me." Arlie tucked the sheet around herself and crawled toward the end of the bed as Samuel approached the cheval mirror.

"I've got it." He gave her his back, not wanting to see the disappointment creeping into her sleep-creased features.

"What's wrong?" she asked.

"Nothing."

This time, there was no doubt that she registered the coolness in his tone. He watched her in the mirror as the lingering fondness melted from her like a light dusting of snow.

"Look." Her eyes darted from him to the door, as if measuring how likely she was to prevent his escape. "Last night, I felt something I haven't felt in a really long time."

Samuel's heart sank, though he had been bracing himself for this since his brain had clicked on. This was the part where he was supposed to tell her he felt it too. That being with her had been like coming back to the home he had never known but always wanted.

He wouldn't.

Arlie shifted, settling back against the pillows again. "The truth is, I haven't been entirely honest with you. And I can't let things go any further between us without you knowing everything there is to know."

The fear he had sensed the morning of her interview returned. Worry tightened her features.

Instinctively, he had already known there was something that she wasn't telling him, but at the time, it hadn't mattered. It hadn't mattered because the only reason she was being hired was to drive his brother to make a colossal mistake that would get him thrown out of Kane Foods and out of Samuel's way.

Now, it didn't matter because things couldn't go any further between them. It was an absolute impossibility.

"There's no need." Looping the last knot on his tie, Samuel snugged it against his neck. For reasons he wouldn't want to dissect, this simple gesture brought him comfort. Delivering him closer to something that resembled his normal life.

"No need?" It wasn't the question itself that gutted him. It was the unprotected hope and vulnerability in her voice.

He needed her to be angry at him. To be irate at the way she was being treated. Her pain, her eagerness. They were his kryptonite.

Conjuring his father, he turned to her, hoping he mimicked the appropriate signs of stony disinterest.

"There's nothing to worry about," he said. "We gave in to a simple biological urge. There's no reason whatsoever this should complicate things."

"But last night you said—"

"We were in the heat of the moment." Samuel ran

his hands through his hair, hoping to tame it into some kind of order. "It was an adolescent urge that we didn't have a chance to scratch back then. When you take some time to think about things with a cool head, I'm sure you'll agree that pursuing this any further would be a disastrous choice for us both."

"Think about *what* things?" There were tears in her eyes but he forced himself not to look away.

He took in her beautiful face, realizing she would never again look at him with curiosity, or kindness, or wonder, and certainly not with the kind of desire she'd scorched him with last night.

"Kane Foods has a very strict policy about company romances." It sounded every bit as weak and pathetic as he feared it would.

"You mean *your father* has a very strict policy about company romances," she accused, "especially with the daughters of his disgraced former employees."

"As badly as you need this job, I'd think that would make you even more concerned." Samuel turned from her, ducking slightly to check his reflection in the mirror. "Our personal history notwithstanding."

"And how would you know how badly I need this job?" Her voice was thin ice. Cold, brittle, imminently dangerous.

Samuel said nothing.

"You researched me," Arlie said accusatorially. "Didn't you?"

"I perform due diligence on all potential hires." Retrieving his phone from the nightstand, a high, static buzzing bloomed in his ears. Twenty-three unread messages.

She stepped down from the bed, the rumpled sheet

around her somehow lovelier and more striking than a couture gown.

"And because I'm so hard up for work, I'll just pretend last night never happened. Is that it?"

That wasn't it *at all*, but he couldn't bring himself to say the words circling inside his head like a horde of hornets.

*I only hired you to get rid of Mason.*

*I had effectively erased you from my memory.*

"That isn't it," he said.

"What is?" she asked.

He could turn his back and leave. Now. Right this second. Give her no answers. No explanations. Let her think the worst.

He faced her.

"When I'd heard what my father said to you—"

"That's what this was?" she asked bitterly. "An apology? Believe me, Samuel Kane, I got used to that treatment from him a long time ago, and didn't need your pity."

"That's not what—"

"Even so, I'm surprised you'd deign to sleep with me after what happened at *Gastronomie*. You're aware of that, I'm assuming?"

Samuel blinked at her. There were many things he hated, but being blindsided ranked near the top. "They didn't."

"Corporate espionage. That's what got me fired from my previous company."

Samuel's mouth opened. Closed. Opened again.

"Does that surprise you?" Arlie paced the length of the room, the sheet trailing behind her like the train on a wedding dress. "We settled out of court, so I imagine it didn't appear on whatever records you perused before reaching out to me."

She was right about that. Her background check had revealed a severely compromised credit score and a legion of late payments, but was otherwise unremarkable.

"The best part is, I'm not the only one who knows about it." A sarcastic smile twisted her lips. "Taegan Lynch? That night on the yacht, she demanded that I either get her information about Project Impact, or she'd go straight to your father."

Memories of that night flashed across Samuel's mind. Arlie's initial flinch. Her fear. Her sadness.

His gut churned and he tasted bile boiling up from his empty, acidic stomach. "Did you give her what she wanted?"

She ceased her pacing to look him squarely in the eye. "No."

The tightness in his chest eased slightly.

"But I thought about it," she said. "I thought about how tired  —" Her voice broke on the word as her shoulders sagged. As if the admission increased rather than lightened the burden. "How tired I am of being afraid. Of thinking about all the ways things can go wrong. Of feeling like no matter what I do, I'll never get out of a mess I didn't even know I was making."

Samuel wanted to comfort her so badly that his bones ached. Wanting to gather her against him. To feel her shoulder blades in the cage of his arms. To feel the crown of her head warm against his chin.

"What do you mean, you didn't know?" he asked.

Arlie didn't answer. Only shuffled over to the laptop bag next to her bed and withdrew a manila folder that she pushed into his hands.

"Here," she said. "Here's what Taegan wanted. Fire me, tell your father whatever you need to tell him where I'm concerned."

Hypocrite that he was, Samuel hadn't yet decided what that would be.

Samuel absorbed this as stolidly as he could under the circumstances, wanting to comfort her so badly that his bones ached. Wanting to gather her against him. To feel her shoulder blades in the cage of his arms. To feel the crown of her head warm against his chin.

They stood squared off for the space of several breathless moments.

"You better go," she said, letting the sheet drop and sauntering stark naked to the bathroom. "I need to get ready for our clients this afternoon."

With the folder in hand, he unlatched her door and rested against it, trying to regain his composure before setting off down the hall.

He walked exactly three steps before stopping to thump his forehead against the wall.

"I thought our nanny broke you of that habit when you were six."

Samuel's spine stiffened as the unmistakable *cocktails in Barbados* voice of his twin floated to him. Gathering what he could of his tattered pride, he reluctantly turned to Mason.

His brother was perfectly dressed and irritatingly fresh-faced, looking like he'd woken from a twenty-year-long nap.

"Good to see you, Mason," Samuel said. "And by the way, thanks for overseeing that photo shoot yesterday."

Mason raised a curious eyebrow. "Now, I knew you

aced your MBA, but I didn't know passive-aggressive 101 was part of your program."

"I made a very simple request," Samuel said. "You gave me your word. Not that I expected it to mean much."

"Maybe I just didn't think that Arlie needed my supervision. Maybe I trusted in her talent and expertise and felt like my attentions were better used elsewhere."

"What's elsewhere's name?" Samuel asked.

From the subtle flinch in Mason's features, Samuel judged that he'd hit his mark. "See you at Fort Funston."

Only when Mason was halfway down the hall did Samuel call after him.

"Are you actually going to be there, or will our father be making apologies on your behalf?"

Mason paused, his back still to Samuel, fingers flexing briefly at his side.

Once, just once, Samuel wished Mason would argue with him. Cite logic. Provide facts. Address his concerns and refute them without humor, without the slippery defense he was so famous for. Just once, he wished they could have an actual conversation about the life they had shared since their arrival on the planet. He wished Mason would tell him to fuck off. Would acknowledge him in any real and lasting way.

"Wouldn't miss it," Mason said, flashing his unnaturally white smile.

# Twelve

The next few days were a whirlwind of activity, and frankly, Arlie was grateful for the distraction. Her arrival in the vast convention hall was like a metaphor for what her insides currently felt like. Cavernous, scooped out, full of empty echoes.

Samuel had successfully avoided her entirely since he'd fled from her suite like he was being pursued by a pack of wild dogs.

Not that she could blame him. What had happened between them was disastrous in every way, particularly in light of his revelation about company romances.

But then, Samuel had made it abundantly clear that their having a romance was nowhere in the cards. One life-changing night of the best sex she'd ever had, yes.

Any kind of lasting connection, forget about it.

She hadn't given herself much time to think about

it. Thinking seemed like an extremely dangerous thing to do right now. Her meeting with Taegan was scheduled for this evening, and Arlie intended to disappoint.

And then there was the matter of Mason.

With Samuel conspicuously absent at all the Kane Foods' meetings and mixers, she'd found herself chatting with Samuel's carefree twin instead. At each and every event, he'd been nothing but warm, attentive, and ridiculously charming.

Fun. Light and playful.

Everything his brother was not.

At last night's dinner, he'd offered to come early to keep her company at the booth this morning, where she was tasked with personally curating the displays of Kane Foods' staggeringly diverse offerings.

She'd been intensely focused, pawing through an entire box of high-fiber cereal to find a handful of perfect flakes, when Mason arrived, paper coffee cups in hand.

"Sustenance," he said, offering her an easy smile.

Arlie set down her pair of tweezers and gratefully took a cup. Lifting it to her lips, she was surprised when the familiar aroma of her favorite vanilla-cinnamon latte drifted upward. She looked up at Mason. "How did you know?"

He grinned at her, taking a sip from his own cup. "As much as I would love to take credit, I texted Charlotte."

"Ah," Arlie said, everything making much more sense. "Charlotte is kind of amazing."

"She definitely is." Popping the white lid from his cup, Mason blew the column of steam away from the liquid.

"And kind of a knockout," Arlie added, stealing a covert glance at him.

"I suppose," he said, shrugging. "If you like that whole naughty librarian kind of thing."

"Do you?" She hadn't meant to ask this question. But some irritatingly hopeful part of her had to know if there was a chance that Charlotte's ridiculously obvious crush on Mason Kane had any hope of being reciprocated.

"Miss Banks," Mason said, mimicking Samuel's stiff formality with alarming precision, "I'm not sure that's an entirely work-appropriate question."

"Since when has that mattered to you?" Arlie aimed her best "we're all friends here" conspiratorial smile at him.

"A good point well made, *Miss Banks*." He took another sip, glancing around them as if he feared the CIA might be watching. And maybe they were. Arlie wouldn't put it past Parker Kane. "Charlotte is incredibly capable, obviously lovely, and totally off limits."

"You forgot *completely enamored with you*."

Shit.

She hadn't meant to say that either.

But the abrupt shift in Mason's features made it entirely worthwhile. He didn't seem like a man easily surprised, but this right here was a complete and total revelation.

"Charlotte?" he asked, handsome features an unconvincing mask of feigned surprise. "What makes you think that?"

The fact that he wanted to know spoke volumes. In Arlie's experience, people only asked this question when they hoped the answer was true.

"Please," Arlie said. "She can barely look at you."

"Since when was that an indicator of interest?" Mason swirled the contents of his cup.

"Since shy girls landed on the planet," Arlie said.

Another dazzling grin. "I never would have guessed."

"Would you have guessed that she writes romance novels?"

*Shit.*

Arlie had been sworn to secrecy, and she was flagrantly dishonoring the pact. She wasn't sure exactly which part of her was hoping for a happy ending for Charlotte when her own was completely out of reach.

"Romance novels?" Mason asked, his eyes keen with interest.

"Yup," Arlie nodded. "Exceptionally well-written. And very…passionate."

Mason's knuckles went white as a fish belly as he lifted the coffee to his mouth. "Speaking of passionate, how was he?"

Arlie coughed, grateful she'd swallowed before latte foam could spray from her lips. "How was who?"

"Paul Martine." Mason slouched against one of the towering walls of the twenty-foot-tall display. "My spies tell me he's notoriously temperamental."

Relief swept like a cool breeze across Arlie's stinging conscience.

"Well, he didn't disappoint. But I think his assistant is going to need some serious therapy."

"I'm sorry I couldn't be there. I had a last-minute emergency to take care of." A shadow passed over Mason's features, gone as quickly as it had arrived.

"Not a big deal." Arlie shrugged. "Samuel stepped in."

"That sounds like him," Mason smirked. "How did you like Willow Creek Villa?"

"Pretty amazing," Arlie said. "Only your father seemed surprised to see me there."

"And by *surprised*, I'm guessing you mean he reacted like he'd just found a rat in his vichyssoise?"

Arlie blinked up at him. She hadn't expected that Mason was at all familiar with this side of his father, as much as she'd watched him lavished with attention.

"Accurate description," she admitted.

"You can't let that bother you. Since Mom died, it's like he wants to personally snuff out every bit of joy in the world."

"I don't remember him being especially pleasant before that."

"He wasn't," Mason said, looking as thoughtful as Arlie had ever seen him. "Forgive the trite metaphor from my favorite subject, but they were like a mixed drink. Mom was the soda and Dad was the scotch. She made him lighter, palatable. Smoothed his sharp edges."

Arlie understood more about that dynamic than she would have liked.

"Speaking of," Mason looked furtively around, withdrawing a flask from his pocket. He lifted it to his lips then offered it to Arlie.

If Samuel was a lost boy, then Mason was Peter Pan.

"It's two thirty in the afternoon," she said, glancing down at her phone. Only to find a new message from Taegan.

You better have something good for me.

"Conference rules," Mason said. "Some of the attendees come from India and Japan. It's already tomorrow there."

Not wanting to compromise their growing bond, Arlie took the flask and brought it to her lips for a quick tug.

Bourbon.

And good bourbon at that. It scalded a smooth, hot channel of brightness all the way to her empty stomach, suffusing her limbs with a pleasant, warm heaviness. She handed the flask back to him just as her phone began to ring in her pocket.

Fearing it was Taegan, she reached down to retrieve it, her stomach flipping when she read the name on the screen.

"It's Kassidy," she said to Mason, searching for a spark of recognition. "My best friend from high school?"

Without a word, Mason swiped the phone from her and answered, pressing the icon to set it on speaker. "If it isn't Kassidy *the brain* Nichols." He paused, lifting a mischievous eyebrow. "I'm corrupting your friend."

There was a beat of silence on Kassidy's end, through which Arlie could actually feel her friend sifting her mind's considerable database.

"I've been trying to do that for years, Mason Kane," Kassidy said. Arlie thought she detected a hint of flirtation in her tone. "She need bail money yet?"

"Not yet," Mason said, "but the day is young. Congratulations on your boutique, by the way. Marlowe tells me there's a line of desperate Philadelphia housewives down the block on any given Tuesday."

"What Botox and a butt lift won't give them, I will."

"Now there's ad-worthy copy right there. Let me know if you're ever in the market. Kane Foods needs more smart people." Mason winked at Arlie.

"Duly noted." Kassidy gave him a polite laugh. "Say, is Miss Arlington Banks at liberty to speak?"

"She is and she shall." Taking the phone off speaker, Mason handed it over to her.

With an apologetic smile, Arlie held up her finger to indicate she'd only be a moment. She stepped away from the booth so she could have a degree of privacy.

"Hey, there," Arlie said, trying to sound like a woman who definitely hadn't had illicit sex with one of the Kanes recently.

"You kissed him, didn't you?" The accusation stung in Arlie's ear.

"Absolutely not. Mason and I—"

"Not Mason," Kassidy said. "Samuel."

How did she know these things? "Technically, he kissed me."

"What else?" Kassidy asked.

"What do you mean?"

"What else did you do?"

Arlie could feel the first fine beads of sweat springing out on her forehead. Suddenly she was transported back to the principal's office, the cracked, faux-leather bench biting into the backs of her thighs.

"I…well…" she sputtered, her cheeks growing hot and red.

"Jesus tailgating Christ. You *slept with* him?"

"Again, technically—"

"Are you actively out of your goddamned mind?"

"Look, it's not like I planned on this happening. I ran into Parker Kane the other morning and he was a complete ass to me. Then Mason didn't show at the photo shoot and Samuel stepped in and the photographer wanted to use us as models and he was holding me and it brought back us kissing on the yacht and—"

"You kissed Samuel on the yacht five days ago and you said nothing to me?" Kassidy's voice had taken on the steely edge that Arlie recognized as part anger and part calculation. "Since when did you keep secrets from me?"

Guilt crushed Arlie's chest.

"I'm sorry," she said. "I don't even know who I am anymore." Her throat tightened as tears thickened her voice, stinging in her eyes. Glancing around the corner, she saw Mason looking in her direction. Arms folded, an expression of concern on his untroubled features.

"You're my best friend." These words were a rescue buoy, a life raft, tossed out by the one person in the world who had once known everything about her. "You've been through a river of bullshit lately and you're going to come out clean on the other side."

Arlie chuckled through her tears in spite of herself. "You stole that from *Shawshank Redemption*."

"Is there someone better than Morgan Freeman to humanize a desperate situation?"

"Thank you for making a joke." Sniffing, Arlie dabbed at the corners of her eyes. "I really am lucky to have you in my life."

Kassidy made a rude noise. "Save that sentimental crap. When you get back, I want details. Length. Girth. Technique. And next time—"

"There will be no next time." As she said it, the memory of Samuel's cool, impenetrable visage floated through her mind. How stupidly hopeful she had been, waking to find him in her bed. Believing it had meant as much to him as it had to her. How quickly and effectively he'd made it clear that she'd been wrong.

"Mmm-hmm."

"Really, Kassidy. This could be very bad for both of us. In a lot of ways."

"Bad is what makes it good."

God, was she right about that.

"Look," Arlie said. "I need to get back to the booth."

"Grope Mason for me."

"Somehow I think that would only serve to further complicate my current situation." Arlie nodded at a passing conference attendee who seemed overly interested in her tear-stained face.

"You seem to like complicated."

It really was irritating, this ability of Kassidy's to be right all the damn time.

"I better go," Arlie said. "I love you."

"Love you too."

Arlie disconnected, holding the phone against her chest, trying without much success to return her heartbeat to normal speed.

"Everything okay?" Mason appeared at her elbow, flask in hand, eyes curious.

"Is anything ever really okay?" she asked.

Mason lifted the flask in her direction. An inexplicable tide of gratitude swept through her as she accepted it and took a greedy pull.

"Completely essential as part of convention survival," he said. "At least until cocktail hour."

"Can I ask you something?"

"As long as higher calculus isn't involved." Retrieving the flask, Mason took a nip as well.

Arlie paused, knowing her question came from a

place inside her she didn't especially like. A hurt, aching need for validation born directly of Samuel's stinging rejection.

"What was it you liked about me in high school?"

Watching Mason's smile unfold was a little like witnessing a sunrise.

He tucked the flask back in his pocket and leaned against the wall next to her. There was something so incredibly surreal about looking at a face so like Samuel's, and so completely different.

"You're going to force me to admit something very unflattering about myself."

"I couldn't imagine that such a thing exists." The bourbon had made Arlie bold and more relaxed than she could remember in a very long time.

"Our father didn't believe in anything as frivolous as an allowance. So if you didn't work, you didn't have money to spend."

"Sounds like him," Arlie said, trying to keep the bitterness from creeping into her voice.

"Well, Samuel always worked and was unwise enough to keep part of his stash in his sock drawer. Enterprising lad that I was, I would make occasional raids to help myself to his resources."

"You *stole*?"

"I like to think of it as self-authorized loans." Mason rewarded her with a mischievous sideways grin. "Anyway, it was on one of my covert entrepreneurial excursions that I happened to discover a sonnet written to a certain someone." A subtle lift of his eyebrow and incline of his head let her know in no uncertain terms who that someone was.

Her.

Samuel had written a sonnet to her.

"And thus we come to the unflattering part. I knew damn well Samuel wouldn't summon the stones to make a go for you, but thought that maybe if *I* did, he might be galvanized into action. Given his lifelong dislike for my general person."

"Let me get this straight. *You* were never really interested in me?"

"I mean, of course I was. I was a teenage boy and you were an attractive and available female. But no, our being an item wasn't my primary motive."

She wasn't sure if it was the afternoon booze or the swirling array of flashing lights and colorful flags of the booths around them, but Arlie began to feel a little dizzy.

Several portions of her personal history had now been rewritten over the past couple weeks.

"Well," Arlie said, leaning back against the wall in a mirror of Mason's posture. "That's a surprise."

"I'm full of them." He glanced out into the maze of booths.

"Which is why I was never quite able to figure out why you're your father's favorite. No offense."

"None taken." Mason was quiet for a long time before he continued.

"When someone looks up to you, wants to be like you, at some point, you actually have to decide whether that admiration is deserved.

"For my father, I think it was easier to make Samuel feel like he didn't measure up than to admit that deep down, my father knows he isn't the kind of man anyone should try to emulate."

Arlie let this sink in, feeling a twinge of pity for the

boy Samuel had been. For the pain and disappointment he must have endured.

"As to my being the favorite," Mason continued, "I don't think I actually am."

"I'm going to need you to elaborate on that," she said.

"He doesn't praise me because he truly thinks I've earned it. Or defend me because he really approves of my behavior."

"Then why does he?" Arlie asked.

"Because it's easy. When he looks at me, he doesn't see a better version of himself. A man he wanted to be and isn't." This was not *at all* how Arlie had imagined this conversation going. "Have you ever talked about this with Samuel?"

Mason laughed. "What are the chances that Samuel would be interested in my assessment of his relationship with our father? Or with anyone, for that matter?"

"I don't know," Arlie mused. "You're the closest thing to a mirror he has. And for what it's worth, you're a lot more insightful than you like to let on."

The brightness of his countenance dimmed incrementally. "Sometimes it's easier to let people believe that they know you."

"I used to think I knew Samuel," Arlie said, unsure why she was dumping all of this in his lap. "Apparently I was incorrect."

"What makes you say that?" Mason nodded to a group of ever-seductive *booth babes* that various companies employed for the purpose of luring onlookers.

"Millhaven Foods." Ever since Taegan had dripped this particular poison into her ear, Arlie couldn't evict the story from her head.

"Who told you about that?" Mason asked.

She briefly debated giving him the full rundown of everything that had transpired between her and Taegan, but the very idea of it made her want to crawl under her bed. "That's not especially important."

"Did this person also tell you that Samuel personally paid for the college funds of all four Millhaven siblings out of his own pocket?" Mason asked.

Arlie blinked at him, this information nearly rocking her off her sensible ballet flats. "No, they didn't happen to mention that."

Mason rounded the corner and strolled back toward the area where she'd been diligently sorting through her cereal earlier. "Did they tell you he established a Millhaven scholarship at Harvard?"

"Also no."

"That's because Samuel went to great lengths to keep his efforts secret after he learned exactly what our father's plans for the company were." Mason retrieved his coffee cup and lifted it to his lips.

Arlie wasn't certain how to feel about this information. After what had transpired between them in the hotel room, she had reminded herself of this every time she began to feel the stirrings of regret. A longing for that conversation to have ended differently.

Making a monster of him had been her best hope at survival.

And now this.

"I appreciate your sense of familial loyalty, but if this is some sort of misguided bid to redeem your brother, I'm afraid it isn't going to work." Lifting her tweezers from the silky gray surface of the counter, Arlie examined the flakes in her *keep* pile, finding one the proper shape and shade to add to the bowl.

"I wasn't aware he needed redeeming."

"Let's just say that pretty much every single encounter I've had with Samuel has ended badly." Technically not a lie. Not the complete truth either.

"Do you think there's any chance that he might still have feelings for you?"

Mason's words were like a sucker punch to the gut. And it stung to know that she wished the answer was yes. "Would it matter if he did? I was under the impression that your father vehemently disapproved of company romances."

A sly smile curled up the corners of Mason's mouth. "So you're saying that if my father weren't against company romances, this information *would* matter?"

Arlie's cheeks flooded with stinging heat. Tricky bastard.

"No," she said. "I'll admit to having a teenage infatuation once upon a time, but—"

Mason laughed. A sound so rich, warm and contagious that she had to fight to keep a straight face. "Watching you invent excuses to walk past the library was my actual hobby for three years."

"Look, a lot has changed since then." Which was the understatement of the century.

"How about this?" he said, taking another slurp from his white cup. "Samuel's been a cold, bossy dick to you ever since you started. Isn't there even the smallest part of you that wants to see how he would react if he thought that you and I were actually an item?"

Oh, the part of her wasn't small.

"Maybe," she admitted.

"Okay," he said. "Hear me out. My brilliant teenage plan had one fatal flaw."

"And that would be?" Arlie asked.

"You weren't participating."

"I don't follow." She paused, the pointy silver tips of her tweezers hovering above the cereal pile. She hadn't expected this question.

"As long as he didn't think you were interested in me, he had no reason to intervene." Mason walked around the long, rectangular high-top table where they'd later be plying potential customers and investors with free booze and alluringly packaged samples. "Should he get the idea that you might return my affections…" He trailed off.

Mason's enthusiasm was nothing if not infectious. "How would you propose we do that?"

Glancing stealthily from side to side, he stepped close to her, his finger warm beneath her chin as he tilted her face up to his.

She had to admit, for the briefest of moments, she could comprehend Charlotte's fascination. Mason was an unreasonably attractive human. Extravagantly indulgent. Fireworks in February. Flash and dazzle and blindingly bright solar flares.

Mason ran a thumb over his lips. "We pretend."

"And what would the end goal be for this particular game of pretend?" she asked, butterflies slam-dancing in her stomach.

"One of two things is going to happen. *A*, Samuel cops to the fact that he's had a thing for you since we were kids. Or *B*, we revenge-annoy the ever-loving shit out of him. Either way, sounds like a good time to me." He wiggled his eyebrows lasciviously.

Arlie wasn't especially proud to admit that her preferred outcome would be *C*, all of the above.

"Mason Kane." She held out her hand for him to shake. "You have a deal."

Instead, he threaded his fingers through hers and swung her hand by his side as he would if they were happy couple, out for a walk.

Arlie looked at him, eyebrow raised in question.

"Practice makes perfect," he said.

"That's such a Samuel thing to say." A subtle pang of sadness constricted Arlie's chest.

"Our supplier appreciation event at Fort Funston is this evening. Any chance you'd like to come help me navigate those treacherous sand dunes?"

"I'd be delighted," Arlie said, surprised to realize that this was true.

# Thirteen

Samuel Kane was in a hell of his own making.

Which was the worst kind of hell, as far as he could figure.

The insultingly beautiful setting only served to intensify his growing displeasure. The sky was something his mother would have painted. Clementine orange, grapefruit pink, the darkening purple of good table grapes.

Sunset.

Beautiful, breathtaking sunset.

And Samuel, forced to host an event for people he mostly couldn't stand.

The cars had arrived in a steady procession, a helpful line of flags guiding guests over the shifting beige terrain of Fort Funston's sand dunes to a hospitality tent. At its center, Charlotte Westbrook handed out name badges behind a fold-out table as the wait staff wove their way through the buzzing crowd with trays of champagne and hors d'oeuvres.

Samuel stood among them, flagrantly breaking his own rule about drinking on the job as soon as he'd seen Mason involved in a tête-à-tête with none other than Arlington Banks.

Sipping the cold, acidic bubbles, Samuel wondered why champagne had become synonymous with celebration when really, it was just overly assertive white wine.

The fact that he'd already downed two glasses had nothing to do with how Mason and Arlie looked annoyingly perfect together, as if they'd actively coordinated their outfits. Mason in his cargo pants and white polo shirt and Arlie in her curve-hugging khakis and cleavage-revealing white tank top. Of course, the invitation had encouraged attendees to "dress for adventure" but this bordered on precious.

As if on cue, a staccato burst of Arlie's laughter floated through the air, and she reached out and touched Mason's bicep. The look of delight on his brother's face threatened to make Samuel crush the champagne glass in his tensed fist.

At that very moment, Charlotte appeared at Samuel's side, a comforting, silky specter in her sensible slacks and snug white T-shirt. "Did you want to welcome everyone?"

They had discussed this in far more rational times.

Samuel glanced at his watch. It was time.

Looking out at the crowd, he had never felt more irritated. Here for the free booze and free food. A bored, stupid assortment of moneyed assholes completely of his father's choosing.

Afterward, he couldn't remember a single word of what he'd spoken. Some ripe bullshit about being honored by their presence and excited for their partnership.

At this point, he nodded to Charlotte, who came forward with a clipboard and pained grimace.

He knew she hated this.

Being the center of attention. Being forced to make announcements. To command the room.

Of course, that hadn't stopped his father from putting Charlotte in any and every situation that required her to overcome this particular "character weakness."

Noticing her distress, Samuel had been on the point of shouting the crowd down when Mason stuck two fingers in his mouth and whistled in the eardrum-puncturing way he'd had when gathering his cronies across the high school courtyard.

"Hey!" Mason called when everyone had fallen silent. "This lovely lady needs your attention."

Charlotte broke into a grateful smile as she blushed a deep rosy red.

*Interesting.*

"We have a total of twelve dune buggies," Charlotte said, pointing to the row of red-and-black vehicles fitted out with flags bearing the Kane Foods' logo for the occasion. "I'm going to read off the pairs of names. Please find your partner and choose your vehicle."

Samuel had mostly tuned her out, draining the last of his champagne when she came to the final pair.

Mason Kane and Arlie Banks.

Which, of course, was exactly how Samuel had told her to set it up.

Mason and Arlie's faces were mirror reflections of delighted surprise as they gave each other a high five.

Together, they strolled down the line, stopping at the second-to-last buggy from the end.

After a brief but amicable exchange, it was Arlie, not Mason, who slid into the driver's seat. Mason leaned forward, his forearm grazing across her breasts as he pointed out the various knobs and wheels.

Now Samuel didn't just want to crush his glass. He wanted to chew it.

"GlowFit didn't show," Charlotte said, presenting her pen-scratched list to Samuel, who couldn't seem to tear his attention away from his twin brother and Arlie buckling themselves in. "It looks like we have one dune buggy left over."

"I'll take it," Samuel said.

Charlotte blinked at him, alarm in her eyes. "But you said you didn't—"

"I changed my mind." Sand shifting beneath his dress shoes, Samuel strode over to the unoccupied buggy, giving Mason a stiff nod as he passed. He settled himself into a leather seat warmed by the coastal sun, buckling his safety belt before reviewing the control panel.

Though he'd had no intention of participating in this activity, he'd studied the design of the dune buggies, lest conversation required him to appear familiar with the configuration.

"Okay," Charlotte called. "We have gifts for all riders, but the first team to find the Kane Foods' swag chest will receive two round-trip tickets to St. Bart's." There was an enthusiastic, champagne-fueled swell of applause. "On your mark. Get set. Go!"

The choppy sound of engines firing up drowned out

the contestants' chatter and, one by one, the vehicles peeled out of the starting gate.

Arlie and Mason shot off, sand spraying from behind their knobby tires like a particulate rainbow.

Samuel followed suit, ghosting a safe distance behind them as they disappeared over a hill and into the endless beige sea.

Arlie glanced back and, seeing him there, stepped hard enough on the gas to make Mason grip the foam-covered black frame.

Samuel felt an unfamiliar sense of acceleration, gooseflesh crawling across his skin as he matched their speed. Wind whipped his hair into a wild frenzy, the white and green ocean beyond providing an auditory backdrop to the ripping motor in this frenzied pursuit.

Chasing them up a steep embankment, he paused in pure wonder as, cresting it, they caught air, the thinnest slice of azure sky appearing between their tires and the sand.

A part of him he didn't entirely like delighted in the fact that Mason hadn't yet relinquished his grip on the frame. He and his brother were afraid, but for entirely different reasons.

Samuel lost them as they disappeared below the horizon.

He stomped on his gas pedal and his vehicle lurched forward as the steering wheel tugged hard to the left. Too late, he realized that he hadn't hit the jump at the same spot. His front guards hit a sand bar, his wheels locking up as his body and the back of the buggy continued their momentum. The strange gravitational shift seemed to unfold in slow motion.

And a sudden memory overtook him. Not yet five

years old, he'd allowed Mason to talk him into concealing himself in a tractor tire during a game of hide-and-
seek. He'd only just become comfortable when Mason
and a group of his friends had decided that rolling the
tire down the steep hill toward Lake Hetherington
would be great fun.

Samuel's recollection of the event returned to him
with sickening accuracy as the horizon inverted, sky
becoming ground, ground becoming sky. He tumbled
end over end, the seat belt biting into his neck and torso,
grit between his teeth, his breath knocked entirely away.

The last thing he heard before a black-velvet blanket
fell over the world was the high, clear sound of Arlie's
scream.

# Fourteen

It was refreshing, this panic.

It meant Arlie didn't need to think about herself.

If she had to identify the chief emotion governing her consciousness at that precise moment, she would have named it guilt. Her charade with Mason had worked just a little too well. They'd poured it on pretty thick. This she couldn't deny.

Mason handing her slim flutes of champagne.

Mason helpfully affixing the name tag just a smidge too close to her breast.

Mason pushing a stray hair away from her face.

Truth be told, she'd already known that Samuel had opted out of the dune buggy event. A couple friendly emails between her and Charlotte had given her pretty much all the information she had needed.

So when he'd volunteered to take the unoccupied

dune buggy, Arlie had been equal parts elated and disturbed.

Had she wanted him to be jealous? *Definitely*. Had she wanted him to risk life and limb? *Not so much*.

She'd made her apologies to Mason and Charlotte, who had looked at her with confusion when she'd insisted on riding in the ambulance with Samuel. In the back of the rocking vehicle, against the beeping of machines and wailing of sirens, she'd listened closely to the EMTs as they systematically checked each part of his body, hoping for any helpful scrap of information about his condition.

They'd managed to get an IV into his arm, and, after determining the source and severity of Samuel's pain, poked a small syringe of Dilaudid into the port.

Seeing Samuel's creased forehead go peaceful and slack with the intervention of the drug drained a measure of tension from her heart.

Arlie leaned over him, gently sweeping sand away from his cheekbone. With the hand not bound by the IV, Samuel reached up, capturing her fingers in his. Looking her in the eye, he squeezed them once.

Once they'd reached the hospital and waited two hours to be seen, the final verdict was completely underwhelming. Samuel had fractured his left collarbone. Luckily for him, it wasn't a compound break, which might have required surgery. Unluckily, he'd need to be trussed up like a roasting hen in a sling for the next six weeks.

"I'll send you home with some pain medication for the next few days, but I'd recommend that you follow up with your regular physician as soon as possible." The very young, visibly exhausted doctor looked to Arlie. "Did you have any other questions?"

"I don't," she said. "Samuel?"

Samuel, propped in the narrow hospital bed, wearing slacks and a hospital gown to replace the shirt they'd cut away in the ambulance, shook his head no.

Arlie thanked the doctor and turned to Samuel when he'd left.

"I'm just going to step out and make a couple calls, okay?"

He gave her an endearingly wobbly thumbs-up.

In the hallway smelling of antiseptic and floor wax, she first called Mason to update him on Samuel's condition and then called Charlotte, who insisted on sending a car service to collect them.

A mere fifteen minutes later, Arlie received a text informing her their car had arrived and was waiting at the emergency room exit.

Samuel insisted on walking, declining the offered wheelchair.

Together, they shuffled out to the curb where a bear of a man with a short, gray ponytail and a dark suit opened the passenger door of a long, black limousine.

Samuel stood next to Arlie, arm in a sling, his affable aspect and dilated pupils springing from the same source.

"Okay," Arlie said. "Let's get you settled."

She looped one hand through his good arm, putting her other on his scalp to make sure he didn't hit his head on the door. Samuel collapsed onto the soft leather seats, his long legs unfolding in front of him as he slid down.

Arlie scooted in after him, giving their driver a nod as he closed the door behind them. On either side of the backbench seat, blue LED-lit ice buckets held an assortment of beers. Behind them, a racked display of mini bottles gleamed beneath a similar glow.

"I'll have one of those," Samuel said, blinking at the gleaming bottles.

"I'm not sure that's a good idea," Arlie said.

"Mason would do it."

The edges of his words had been filed away, leaving Samuel with the soft, damp speech of your average, moderately lubed barfly.

"I don't know that I would trust Mason's instincts in this particular situation," Arlie said.

Squinting at the mini bottle of vodka, Samuel poked at it. "Why is this so small?"

Arlie bit her lip, trying not to laugh. "Factory mistake?"

His head sank back against the headrest, eyelids falling closed as the limousine whisked them through the night. The faraway lights of San Francisco whirred by the tinted windows like a carpet of stars. They weren't going back to the Kanes' personal villa at Willow Creek Winery, but to the large, densely populated upscale hotel Charlotte had booked them into for the conference.

"I've been doing a lot of thinking over the last few days." Samuel's eyes were still closed, his strong jaw drooping slightly.

Arlie's heart fluttered in her chest. "You have?"

"Mmm-hmm," he said. "And I came to a realization. Would you like to know what it is?"

"Sure," she said, not at all positive that she did.

"After careful consideration—" he halted and, for a horrifying moment, Arlie was certain he would either fall asleep or lose his train of thought "—I'm pretty certain that I was in love with you."

It was a good thing she was already sitting down. Every molecule of air abruptly evaporated from the limo's darkened cab. Her heartbeat drummed in her ears, an inexplicable primal pulse deeper than her breath.

"What memory in particular brought you to this conclusion?" she asked when words were finally a thing again.

"Do you remember when Marlowe had a sleepover party for her fifteenth birthday?" He made a passingly fair job of the complex combination of consonants and sibilants. Arlie hoped this might be a promising indicator that the heaviest of the medication was beginning to wear off.

She did remember.

She remembered in alarming detail.

The herd of long-limbed debutantes, all out of braces, save her. Designer overnight bags. The boathouse decorated with throw pillows and blankets of Marlowe's favorite seafoam green.

"I do," she said.

"Before the party, I snuck down to the boathouse, cracked open a couple windows, and found myself a convenient spot in that giant tree in the backyard."

"Hoping to witness a pillow fight?" she asked.

"Maybe," he said. "But then Marlowe had to come back to the main house, and one of the other girls called her a spoiled bitch and started talking about how she'd only accepted the invite so she could try and sneak into Mason's bedroom."

Oh, Arlie remembered just which girl that had been.

Brittany Payne.

At the time, she'd been the youngest up-and-coming prima ballerina for the Philadelphia Ballet. These days, she was a bank teller with three kids in Ardmore.

"But *you*," Samuel said, pointing at Arlie with his good arm. "You stood up and told her that she'd better come down with a sudden mysterious illness and excuse herself or you'd give her a good reason to vanish."

"I said that?" Arlie asked, knowing full well it was true. She had known even as she'd done it that she'd just permanently etched her name on the Lennox Finch social blacklist.

"You did," he said. "And that was it. That was the memory."

Given that any kind of long-term romance between the two of them was a complete impossibility for many reasons, what good did it do her to know this now?

"I'm sorry," Samuel said after her extended silence. "I shouldn't have told you that." His hand landed heavy on the leather seat between them.

Arlie studied it. His neatly trimmed nails. The callus on his thumb where he held his pens. The physical reality of this man who had cut such a broad swath through her life.

Arlie tightened her hand into a fist to keep from reaching out to him.

"No apologies necessary," she said, the realer, truer words she wouldn't allow herself to say stuck somewhere deep inside.

*I'm reasonably certain I loved you, too.*

# Fifteen

If this day had a theme, bottomless humiliation would be it.

First, overturning a goddamn dune buggy. Then a trip to UCSF hospital in a screaming ambulance. And now a stroll through a marble-columned hotel lobby in the hospital gown and torn slacks he'd been sent home in. Sling and all.

The only blessing in this equation, small though it may be, came to him courtesy of one of the most unlikely sources: his father.

Entirely too important to stay in the pedestrian accommodations attached to a convention center, he'd had Charlotte book them all into the Fairmont. Which meant that at least his pilgrimage wouldn't be witnessed by the herds of conference attendees congregated at every available nightly watering hole to get expense-account-wasted after the exhibit hall closed.

"So far, so good." Arlie's grip on the biceps of Samuel's good arm tightened as she steered him past a group of men spilling out of the restaurant, forced laughter ringing through the cavernous space. She was surprisingly strong for her size, and had proved an exceptionally adept aid in getting him into and out of the limousine.

His watery memories of their ride back from the hospital being humiliation number 1,583. Now that the drugs were wearing off and his head clearing, he had the definite feeling his loose-lipped declarations would come back to bite him.

At last, they reached the elevator, where, at his direction, Arlie pressed the button for the twelfth floor. When they arrived, they made their way down the blissfully empty hall to his door. She dug the key card from his wallet and swiped it on the sensor pad.

The cool, quiet blast of air hit them as she flicked on the overhead lights, the lobby's noise and din a thousand miles away.

"Let's get you into bed."

Samuel paused in the entryway, the thought of sliding his sandy and sweaty body into the clean sheets causing a beat of panic to sizzle through his system.

"I can't," he said. "Not until I shower."

Arlie stood before him, her tight white tank top dust-streaked, her cheeks sun-kissed and dappled with freckles, her wind-whipped hair gathered into a hasty tangle at her nape. Concern darkened her wide blue eyes. "You're not supposed to get your sling wet, remember?"

"If I don't get the rest of me wet, there's no way I'm getting in that bed."

She blew a stray hair out of her eyes and scrubbed her hands together with all the determination of a battlefield nurse. "Let me check out our setup here," she said, pushing open the bathroom door.

*Our.*

There was something comforting about the way she said this. Like they were a team.

"Thank God for separate shower/tub combos." Stepping toward the glass-enclosed marble cube, she opened the door and lifted the detachable showerhead out of its holster. "This could work."

"I'm sure I can manage," Samuel said, moving toward the door. "Thank you for all your help today."

She arched an eyebrow at him in a half-bemused, half-insulted smirk. "You're not quite rid of me yet, Samuel Kane."

Re-holstering the showerhead, she turned on the taps, holding a hand in the spray until she was satisfied with the temperature.

"All right, mister," she said, turning to Samuel. "Strip."

"You really don't need to help me with this," he insisted.

"You forget that I've seen you naked. Twice now. There's absolutely no reason whatsoever to be bashful."

Samuel quickly realized that her seeing him naked wasn't the problem at all.

It was his memories of their being naked *together.* Already, his mind had begun an impromptu slideshow. Even through the haze of pain meds, he felt himself developing a problem.

"How about humiliation?" he asked. "Surely I've met my quota for the day."

"This will go quicker if you cooperate." Coming around behind him, she loosened the ties of his hospital gown, first at his neck, then between his shoulder blades. With a kind of expert tenderness, she helped him out of the flimsy garment, tossing it in the trash when she'd successfully liberated his sling-bound arm.

"Shoes," she ordered.

Obediently, Samuel toed off his lace-up dress shoes, sand gritty between the souls of his feet and the cool marble floor. His socks had been lost somewhere in the shuffle.

"This, I can do one-handed," he said, backing away when she reached for his belt.

"I'll bet," she quipped.

Unbelted and unzipped, his pants pooled on the floor at his ankles. All that remained were his boxer briefs, and these, he wasn't sure he could successfully manage on his own without bending his torso.

"What comes up..." With a teasing grin, Arlie hooked her thumbs in the waistband and drew his boxer briefs down his legs.

Samuel wasn't sure if he'd ever felt so naked in all his life.

Luckily, Arlie seemed to pick up on this, keeping her eyes on his as she assessed the situation.

"I think the best option here would be for you to stand facing the mirror. That way your arm is away from the water," she suggested.

"Sounds reasonable." He stepped into the shower, assuming the assigned position as he glanced back at her. "You're going to get soaked."

"Please," she scoffed. Removing her khakis, Arlie followed him into the shower in her panties, bra and tank top, doing her best to step around the water as she reached up and retrieved the shower hose. "I must have participated in a hundred car washes for Debutantes Against Drunk Drivers while we were at Lennox Finch."

"I remember them fondly," Samuel said.

The warm water felt like salvation on his sore screaming muscles as Arlie carefully aimed the nozzle away from his elaborate sling.

Retrieving one of the fluffy washcloths from the shower bench, Arlie held it under the spray. She added a dollop of shower gel and brought the cloth to his skin, working it over his back in long, careful strokes.

Samuel felt tension that had seemed to live within him for years melting beneath her capable hands. Running out of his body and down the drain with the swirling suds.

"That's nice," he said.

And it was.

To be cared for. Looked after. Seen to. Feelings he hadn't experienced at any point in his adult life.

"I'm glad," Arlie said. Reaching around from behind him, she ran the washcloth over his chest, his stomach, pausing when she approached his groin.

"You want to take it from here?" she asked, pressing the cloth into his hand.

"Why?"

Odd how one word could crumble the tenuous wall he'd attempted to build between them. Because he wanted this. He wanted her.

He felt her breath quicken behind him, tickling his spine.

The washcloth skimmed below his belly button and over his cock, her taut nipples pressing into his back through the sodden fabric of her tank top.

"Samuel?" Her voice was warm as melted butter and smoky as good scotch.

"Yes?"

"Can I touch you?"

"Please."

Then the washcloth was gone and a moan he was powerless to contain rose up from the deepest part of him as he glanced down, watching himself slide through her delicate fingers. Leaning forward, he planted one hand on the cool marble wall.

"I need to be clear," she said, a taunting edge to her voice as she brushed her thumb over his rapidly swelling head. "Are we giving in to a simple biological urge?"

He turned, relishing her surprise as he claimed her lips.

She moaned into his mouth, opening to him, allowing his greedy exploration, her tongue stroking over his.

Kissing her felt like falling into the deep end, like drowning, then the first lungful of oxygen after breaking the water's surface.

He couldn't get enough.

The tender curve of her earlobe. The delicate skin of her neck. Her sweet, pearly nipples. The flat, hard place over her wildly beating heart.

"I need to taste you." He cupped her sex, her wet panties against his palm.

Her lush lips curved upward in a small, secret smile as she stripped off her tank top and bra before twisting the shower faucet. The water slowed to a trickle then stopped.

Their wet bodies left a trail over marble and carpet. With her help, he settled himself onto the mattress, his slung arm propped on pillows in the center of the bed.

"Take off your panties."

Her breasts rose and fell with erratic breaths, her nipples tightened into buds above the elegant ladder of her rib cage. She bit her lower lip as she gathered the clammy fabric between her thumb and forefingers and, never breaking eye contact, slid it down the long expanse of her thighs.

"Good," he said. "Now undo your hair."

Arlie pulled her low bun loose, freeing it to spill over her naked breasts as he reached out to her with his good arm. She carefully climbed onto the bed, the whole, beautiful length of her body tense with awareness of him.

Of his pain.

Her eyes darted to his shoulder in its elaborate truss. "Are you sure?"

"Come here." Hand on the small of her back, he guided her upward toward the head of the bed.

The guileless, startled uncertainty on her face when she understood what he wanted only dumped gasoline on the inferno of his desire. Those lovely, flushed, freckled cheeks. The awareness shifting from his body to hers. To what he would do to her.

"That's it, baby," he said.

With her knees on either side of his rib cage, he ran his fingers up one long, pale thigh and down the other.

He could have gone on that way forever.

Watching her stomach tighten every time his finger

slid up the silky skin of her inner thigh. The way her
teeth sank into her pillowy lower lip when he stopped
just shy of her sex, skipping to trace down her opposite leg.

"You want my mouth on you?" he asked, skimming
her sweet, smooth folds with his lips.

"Please," she breathed, eyelids falling closed, dark
lashes feathering her cheeks.

"Tell me," he said.

"I want your mouth on me."

"Look at me while you say it," he ordered.

Her pale lids lifted, an entire azure summer sky
boiled down in her smoldering gaze.

"I want your mouth on me, Samuel."

He eased her down on his chest, drawing her nearer
to his mouth. Bearing her weight, he felt anchored. Real.
An actual person with an existence of his own. Apart
from his father. Apart from his family. Apart from his
identity as a Kane altogether.

Then there was the matter of Arlie Banks. Naked.
Alive. Wanting. Hands gripping the headboard. Her features unbearably open and innocent with expectation.

He wanted to tell her not to show so much. Not to
give so much. But that had never been her. A girl who
wore not just her heart on her sleeve, but her soul also.

Leaning forward, he kissed one freckle on her inner
thigh, then another, following the constellation toward
the source of the most intense pleasure he'd ever known.

He was torturing her and he knew it. But he didn't
want this moment to end. She was Christmas morning. All heady expectation, gifts glistening and yet un-
wrapped. Pure possibility.

As if sensing his hesitation, Arlie slid a hand down

her stomach, long fingers moving through her downy curls and parting the seam of her sex. "I'm so wet for you, Samuel."

Her fingers carried the scent of earth and rain as she dragged them across his lips.

Unable to wait one second longer, Samuel surged forward, splitting her with one long languorous lick.

Her sharp intake of breath felt like it had been stolen from his own lungs.

She was sin and salvation on his tongue. Sweetness and ruin. The most intoxicating combination he'd ever encountered.

If he tasted her from this moment until his dying day, there would never be enough. Dipping the tip of his tongue into her slick folds, he began a slow, deliberate exploration. And while he explored, Samuel did what he had had always done.

He studied.

Memorizing every ripple and curve. Watching to see what made her bite her lip, which places and patterns caused her breath to come faster. All the time, avoiding the hot, sensitive bundle of nerves at her apex.

Arlie's impatient sigh was equal parts eagerness and frustration. Her hips undulating impatiently against him. Her need further swelling his own.

In the end, his motives were as simple and selfish as breathing. He *needed* to see her come undone like he needed air. He wanted her above him, rising like a marble statue in the moonlight, knowing that he had been the cause of something that stripped her worries away.

At last, at *long* last, he flicked her clit with his tongue. She gasped. Her body jerked upright like a sudden electrical current had passed through it. The culmination arriving in a single, sizzling, *"Oh."*

Were he a musician, Samuel would play that note in perpetuity. He would compose an entire symphony with that as his theme. All he wanted in that moment was to hear it again. To hear it always.

Her fingers fisted in his hair, the pain and pleasure from his scalp traveling straight down into his throbbing cock. He slid his tongue over her slick bud, teasing it, memorizing the rhythm of her bliss.

She shuddered over him, her face a mask of concentration as she let herself be taken.

He had meant to draw this out. To bring her to the edge. To pull her back. To drive her as mad as he already felt. But now he couldn't stop. He was lost in his own experience, drinking in her pleasure like soil drinks spring rain.

This was life.

*She* was life.

A rosy flush had broken out over her breasts, glowing from a fine sheen of sweat. Her stomach shuddered, her tawny nipples hard as pearls.

He quickened his pace, letting his tongue vibrate against her core, tasting the earthy nectar of her arousal.

"Samuel—" Her thighs tensed, her eyes flying open as pleasure exploded across her features, scorching the landscape like a bomb.

Samuel would have given his entire inheritance to have a painting made of her the way she looked in that exact moment.

The freedom. The pure, essential reduction of her to a woman and nothing more. A goddess capable of granting madness or bliss with the cosmos unfolding around her and within her.

Arlie went limp, collapsing against the headboard and panting into her own folded arms.

The curtain of hair fell on either side of her face, tickling his cheeks.

Samuel's hand went to the small of her back, wandering upward until it landed at the base of her neck. They looked at each other as her breath slowed, something unsayable passing between them.

Arlie shifted her weight, moving backward until she was kneeling, straddling his hips, hands running over his mounded pectoral muscles and down the ridged washboard of his stomach.

Rocking her hips, she slid up and down his length, pausing to increase the friction when she reached his smooth, swollen head. His fingers dug into her hips, trying to hold on to his control as she teased him. Slowly. Deliberately.

Though the need to be inside her robbed him of all reason, he wanted to let her have this moment, to have dominion over her pleasure as he suspected she had over so few elements of her life.

With a wicked smile twisting her lips, Arlie positioned him between her thighs, keeping her eyes on his as she sank down over him, sheathing him in her satin warmth. Inch by maddening inch.

She was molten hot. Unbearably tight. Immeasurably soft and slick.

"Oh, God," he ground out. "You feel so fucking good."

"Yeah?" she asked, sinking incrementally lower.

Heavy, drugging desire gathered low in Samuel's

groin. Even in his compromised state, it took everything in him not to wrest control of the pace and bury himself in her. "Yes."

With fingers dug into his shoulders, Arlie lowered herself until their bodies met. Her succulent ass against the tops of his thighs.

"You're so beautiful, Arlington Banks." He wondered when the last time was someone told her that. Better not to know, actually. Though Kane Foods' lawyers were East Coast sharks, they were unlikely to be able to get him out of murder charges.

Her eyes flicked away. A quick sidestep of the compliment.

"You are." He lifted his hand to her cheek, guiding her gaze back to his. "You're the most beautiful woman I've ever known."

As if to change the subject, Arlie's hips began a slow, serpentine undulation, moving him inside her.

He let his hand trail from her cheek to the delicate shoreline of her jaw, down her throat and her chest until it found her breast. Brushing her nipple with the pad of his thumb, he felt her contract around him.

It was absolutely unbearable that he couldn't experience her with every atom of his body. That he was held back from devouring her with both hands in addition to his eyes and his mouth.

She shifted, creating space to move her hips up and down his length, letting him slide almost entirely out of her before plunging down on him again. Their flesh met with a wet slap that made him want to break things.

Beginning with her control.

Releasing her nipple, he planted his hand against

her tensed stomach, his thumb dipping down into her desire-dampened curls.

Her lips formed a round *O* of surprise as he teased the nub of flesh already made sensitive by his ministrations.

Her palms against his chest, Arlie leaned forward, their mouths fusing as she quickened her pace. He followed her lead, circling her clit more urgently as she lifted and dropped her pelvis, deepening the delicious friction between them.

Arlie broke their kiss, her lips hot and wet against his ear.

"I wanted you from the first time I saw you reading *Peter Pan* in your father's library." Her hot breath sent shivers flooding down his arm.

She was doing for him what he'd done for her. Telling him their story.

"I've measured every kiss against that night in the closet," she said, punctuating the admission by tracing his earlobe with her tongue.

Desperate to send her over the edge before he lost himself entirely, Samuel gently pinched her clit. A thrill coursed through him as she gasped. Her torso jerked upward as her fingernails dug into his shoulders and she howled her pleasure.

The vision of her like that, head thrown back, lost in pure abandon, was enough to send Samuel spiraling into bliss. A dark, sweet pleasure wrung a cry from his chest. He surged beneath her, lifting them both.

As they eased back down into a stillness interrupted only by the soft sounds of their slowing breaths, Arlie lifted herself off him and gently burrowed against his uninjured side. Her leg thrown over his thigh, the small shell of her ear pressed against his chest, her hand banded around his opposite hip.

In all his years, he'd never experienced anything like this. A woman who fit herself around him with a perfection that denied explanation. Many clichéd metaphors came to mind, most of them involving puzzle pieces, but he rejected them.

"You should have asked me to prom," she said in the sleepy contented cat voice he had already grown to adore.

"I wish I had." He meant it. A long-time student of the butterfly effect, he couldn't help but wonder exactly how their lives would have been different if he could go back and change this one small thing.

"Did you know," she asked, a grin audible in her voice, "that Mason never really had a thing for me?"

An arc of fear punctured the thick of haze of Samuel's pleasure.

"What?" he asked.

"He told me earlier today while we were working on setting up the booth." Her index finger made a solitary voyage up his rib cage, tracing the edge of his sling. "The only reason he ever chased me was because he knew you were too shy to come after me yourself. He thought that, seeing as you mostly disliked him, the prospect of seeing us together might push you to make a move. I guess it finally worked."

Inexplicably, the lights in the room dimmed. Samuel's breath became shallow and quick as his heartbeat accelerated. There was no universe in which this had existed as a possibility in his mind.

That all those years ago, Mason had actually been trying to help him.

All this time, he'd been eaten hollow by his resentment for his own brother.

Driven to work that much harder in hopes their father would finally notice.

In his relentless pursuit to earn what Mason had always been freely given, Samuel had become the very thing he'd hated.

A man blinded by his own grudges.

Just like his father.

And just like his father, he'd set about using people like chess pieces.

People like Arlie Banks.

Guilt and self-loathing scalded him as he registered her warm skin on his. He'd dragged her straight into the swirling eye of the storm without a second thought.

And for what?

Eventual control of Kane Foods? Was it really even about that anymore? Had it ever been?

An avalanche of shame compressed his chest until he could no longer bear it.

"Arlie, there's something I need to tell you."

Her body tensed against him. "What?"

He hesitated, knowing there was no way to make what he was about to say any less terrible than it was.

"I wasn't honest with you about the reason you were invited to interview for a food stylist position at Kane Foods." She sat up, and he instantly missed the sleepy, solid weight of her. Eyes that had looked at him with such yearning only minutes ago were now wide with trepidation.

"The truth is, I've been looking for a way to push Mason out of the company, and I thought that maybe, if I brought you on, Mason might be tempted to break our father's rule."

There were any number of indignities Samuel would have willingly suffered to avoid the wounded look in Arlie's eyes. "You hired me because you hoped your brother would seduce me?"

"Yes," he admitted.

"And what would have happened to me in that scenario?" she asked.

Hearing these words spoken so frankly and directly made him realize how little he'd considered what the world would truly look like for Arlie Banks had his plan succeeded.

She would have been fired, most certainly, but she would have made sure she left with a considerable severance. And maybe his brother as a consolation prize.

Or so he had told himself.

"Never mind," she said, holding up a hand and scooting away.

"Please." Samuel maneuvered himself upright, hot white pain piercing his shoulder. "Let me talk. Just for a minute."

"No." She pushed off the side of the bed and marched across the room, quickly stepping into her panties and fastening her bra. "I don't want to hear anything you have to say."

Samuel covered himself with a blanket and carefully maneuvered to the edge of the mattress. "I know that there's no excuse for what I did or any kind of apology that can make it right. But everything I did, I did before—"

"Before what? You decided that maybe you wanted to sample me before your brother had the chance?"

"It wasn't like that," he said.

"Really?" she asked, yanking her tank top over her sodden bra. "What was it like?"

Words. Treacherous words abandoned him and he sat there in silence as empty and dry as a desert. Try as he might, he couldn't force any of the chaotic thoughts in his head to exit his mouth.

*I didn't know you wanted me like I wanted you.*

*I didn't know Mason was capable of anything like self-sacrifice.*

Disgust twisted Arlie's delicate features. "The other morning, when I confessed what had happened with *Gastronomie*, you could have told me. But you let me stand there, thinking I had taken advantage of this opportunity. You let me believe that I had disappointed you. That *I* was the one who was dishonest."

"I'm sorry," he said, unable to meet her gaze.

"It looks like we both are." Arlie stepped back into her khakis, hastily zipping them before gathering her bag. "There I was, eager for the opportunity when apparently, I didn't do my *real* job to your satisfaction."

"Arlie—"

"I have to hand it to you." She dug her hands into her passion-tangled hair to gather it into an elastic. "That was a pretty impressive little speech last night. Was that just the drugs talking, or are you really capable of deliberately toying with the life of someone you claim to have been in love with once upon a time?"

Samuel forced a breath into his lungs. "It's not just a claim, Arlie. It's a part of my life I made myself forget."

"Must be nice," she said, thunderheads darkening her eyes. "To surgically excise entire portions of your memory. Was this a recent effort? Or did I become an inconvenient part of your history before you decided to use me as bait?"

He looked up at her, deliberately memorizing every detail, knowing that this might very well be the last conversation they'd ever have. "When your mother was fired and Mom died six months later, it was like everything light and good in my world vanished."

Her bitter scowl softened, if only infinitesimally, so he went on.

"I couldn't live in a world where I'd lost that much. So I created one where I'd never had anything worth losing at all. I know it doesn't excuse what I've done, but I meant what I said in the limo. I did love you, Arlie. Before I let myself become a parody of everything I despised, I loved you."

He willed her to believe him.

"I'm sorry for what happened to you, Samuel," Arlie said, waiting until he looked her in the eye. "Just like I'm sorry that your tyrant of a father showered Mason with attention and ignored and criticized you. I'm sorry that you're still letting a man like that run your life. But most of all, I'm sorry that you felt like the best way to fix that was to interfere with mine."

Arlie hoisted her bag onto her shoulder and stalked toward the door.

He yearned to go after her to do or say whatever it took to keep her there, with him. But with him was exactly the last place she should be. For reasons he both knew and wished he could forget, being far away from him was the very best possible thing for Arlie Banks.

He let her go.

The door closed behind her like a gunshot.

# Sixteen

Back to the place where it all began.

Arlie stood in the gleaming chrome elevator, a lump in her throat and Kassidy at her side.

"I really appreciate you coming with me," Arlie said, doing her best to sound grateful and calm rather than gutted and terrified. In her sweaty palm, she clutched the heavy key card Charlotte had been kind enough to add after-hours access to.

"As if I would have let you face this alone." Kassidy huffed, blowing hot air from her nostrils as the muscles in her elegant jaw tightened. "After what Samuel did to you, he better hope we don't run into him."

Arlie was comforted by Kassidy's fury on her behalf. And if her best friend only knew how she had omitted key portions of the events she'd relayed to her. Like the fact that Samuel had fessed up to hiring her as part of a plot to oust Mason from the company only after they'd slept together a second time.

Arlie had returned to the moment she'd left again and again. The sorrowful expression on his face had been scorched into the backs of her eyelids, hanging in the dark when she couldn't sleep. Which had been often over the last few days.

When the initial onslaught of anger at Samuel's revelation had burned out of her system, all Arlie felt was tired. Tired, and sad. A bone-deep, abiding ache that rolled through her like a gray fog, relieving her of all thought and reason.

Taegan hadn't waited long.

The morning after Arlie had failed to show for their rendezvous, she'd received a text letting her know Parker Kane would be receiving a special surprise in the coming days.

Between this development and Samuel's admission, her resigning had seemed like the only logical option. She'd given two copies of her formal letter to Charlotte and asked her to give them to Mason and Samuel after she had a chance to clear out of her office.

The elevator slowed to a stop, the familiar *bing* announcing their arrival on the fifteenth floor.

The doors opened on the gleaming, marbled corridor. In the dim, after-hours light, it almost looked romantic.

"This way," Arlie said, adjusting the empty cardboard box in her arms.

"How much you want to bet that Parker Kane has a 24K gold plunger?" Kassidy said, taking in the opulence of their surroundings. She elbowed her as they walked side by side the last few feet to Arlie's soon-to-be-former office.

Flipping on the light, Arlie set the box down on her desk, pierced by the realization that this beautiful space would soon belong to someone else. Someone who didn't have mistakes like hers trailing behind them like acrid smoke.

"Deep breath." Kassidy gave Arlie's upper arm a gentle squeeze. "You left *Gastronomie* and you survived. You'll survive Kane Foods too."

"I didn't just leave *Gastronomie*. I was fired." The words tumbled from her lips, surprising her. She hadn't had any intention of telling her friend that now.

Kassidy's dark brows jerked up toward the neatly knotted rows of her braids. "Come again?"

Arlie felt a strange sense of relief. There was no going back now. This last artifice would be ripped away, and she would be raw, and tender, but real.

"I was being courted by a different magazine. Over dinner one night, Hugh—the marketing executive I'd been talking to—asked me about my role in tracking food aesthetic trends for a new social media feature we'd been working on. As it happened, it wasn't me he was courting at all—he wanted to steal our idea. The other magazine went live with their social media feature first and when the features editor traced the leak back to me, she accused me of corporate spying."

Kassidy's mouth dropped open in shock. "Oh, shit."

"Yeah," Arlie agreed. "But I swear to God, Kassidy, the way Hugh was talking about it, I didn't think I was telling him anything he didn't already know."

Kassidy nodded encouragingly.

"Anyway, they hired lawyers who found a clause in my confidentiality agreement they could tee off. They tee'd hard and sued me."

"I mean, I can understand firing you, but a lawsuit? That just seems...vindictive. Especially if it was an inadvertent disclosure."

"Well, vindictive isn't exactly an inaccurate description where my former CMO is concerned. Or other colleagues at *Gastronomie,* for that matter." Opening her filing cabinet, Arlie began removing the stacks of glossy portfolios she'd brought with her in more optimistic days.

"Jesus." Kassidy shook her head, looking almost as tired as Arlie felt.

"We settled out of court, but it took most of what I had." Arlie dropped the portfolios in the box and set to work pulling the few files she'd begun to assemble. "All of it, really."

Kassidy blinked at her, eyes glossing over with tears. Arlie could count on one hand the times she'd seen her best friend cry and still have leftover fingers. "Why didn't you tell me?"

Arlie had asked herself this same question at least a hundred times. She didn't like the answer any more than she knew it was absolutely true.

Shame.

She was ashamed that she had let herself be so charmed. So deceived. And beyond that, as the unwealthy girl raised with very wealthy people, the idea of asking anyone in general and her best friend in particular for help pulling her ass out of a self-made fire made her want to crawl into a very deep hole.

Which was essentially what she had done after all.

"I could have helped you." Kassidy reached out and placed her hand over the files Arlie was sifting through, forcing her to pay attention.

"You hated being a lawyer, remember? You said that you would sooner have your fingernails removed than use your considerable mental gifts litigating someone's mistakes."

"We're not talking about *someone*," Kassidy said, taking the files from Arlie and adding them to the box. "We're talking about *you*. I'm still licensed in the state of Pennsylvania and I have *contacts*."

Arlie didn't doubt it. She'd seen firsthand how the best and brightest in every field were drawn like moths to the flame of Kassidy's charisma and intelligence.

"As much as I appreciate the offer, what's done is done. In any case," Arlie sighed, feeling both heavier and lighter all at the same time, "that's why I haven't invited you over to my apartment lately, if you want to know the truth. Because I'm not living there anymore. I moved into a smaller place in Hunting Park. And now that this job is ending, I'll probably lose that too."

Kassidy wrapped an arm around her shoulders. "You'll move in with me."

Arlie shook her head. "I couldn't ask that."

"You're not," Kassidy said. "I'm *telling* you. No way my friend is living in some little shack overlooking a dumpster."

Sliding out of Kassidy's side embrace, Arlie picked up the oversized photography books she'd set up on the small coffee table, needing to be busy. Needing to get this done. "I don't know, Kassidy."

"Come *on*." Her friend broke into a mock whine. "It will be just like the old days. Only we'll be able to drink wine and watch all the naked men we want."

Arlie laughed, remembering the time Kassidy's famously strict father had caught them with a bottle of

Boone's Farm Strawberry Hill and a bootleg Blu-ray of *Blue Lagoon*. They'd both ended up grounded for a month of summer break.

"I'll think about it."

A knock on her office door sent Arlie's heart racing. She turned around slowly, hoping to God she didn't see Parker, or worse—Samuel—standing there.

Thankfully, it was neither.

Mason slouched in the doorframe, handsome and carefree, if a bit rumpled. "Say it ain't so."

So much for Charlotte waiting to give Mason her letter.

"It's so." Arlie cushioned a mug full of pens in her office sweater and nestled the bundle into the box. "All of it."

Crossing the office, Mason dropped into a chair opposite the desk. "Look, what happened between you and Samuel doesn't need to end your employment at Kane Foods."

"I thought my sleeping with your brother was a pretty clear violation of your father's one and only inviolable rule."

"Wait." Mason's tawny brows gathered in the center of his smooth, tanned forehead. "What?"

Arlie's cheeks flamed scarlet. "I... You... What were *you* referring to?"

"After the conversation we had in the convention hall and what happened at the sand dunes, I just assumed—"

"Sand dunes?" Kassidy stopped short, a print of Ansel Adams' *Half Dome* clutched in her hands. "What happened at the sand dunes?"

Mason leaned forward in his chair. "You're saying, you and Samuel—?"

"Try to keep up, Kane," Kassidy interrupted. "There was mutual groping on the yacht and they hooked up at your family's winery. Accurate?" Kassidy cut her eyes to Arlie.

"Yes, but—"

"What we all seem to be unclear about is what went down after the sand dunes. Perhaps Arlie could enlighten us?" Seating herself in the chair next to Mason, Kassidy propped one long, legging-clad ankle on the opposite knee.

So, she did. Describing the ambulance ride, the hospital, her escorting Samuel up to the hotel room afterward. And, at last, coming to the part she really wasn't looking forward to.

She paused, looking Mason in the eye. "I'm afraid this next part might be upsetting. And if you'd rather ask Samuel yourself—"

"I'm a big boy," he said in a flirty tone that might have been for Kassidy's benefit. "I can take it."

Taking a deep breath, she plunged ahead. "That night, at the Fairmont, Samuel told me the real reason he'd hired me."

Genuine confusion etched a crease in Mason's brow. "What do you mean the *real* reason?"

"He was hoping that, given a chance to bag the one conquest who had escaped you, you'd break your father's cardinal rule and get yourself ejected from the company." She glanced nervously at Mason. "Permanently."

Mason huffed a breath, leaning back in his chair. Stripped of his usual cavalier, devil-may-care countenance, the younger Kane looked—dare she say it—thoughtful.

"Samuel went through all that trouble just to get rid of me?"

Arlie observed him carefully, looking for signs of reaction to this information, unsure what to expect.

A frown flickered at the corners of his mouth, but didn't quite land. His eyes unfocused as he contemplated the space beyond Arlie's shoulder.

"I'm sorry," she said. "I should have—"

"No." Mason shook his head emphatically as he stood. "No, this is good."

"Good?" Arlie asked incredulously. "How can this possibly be good?"

"Do you have any idea what it would take for Samuel to break not just *a* rule, but our father's *primary* rule? Plot to overthrow me notwithstanding."

"What do you mean?" Kassidy asked as if reading Arlie's mind.

"I just mean that there may be hope for him yet." Mason scratched his jaw, sandpapery with stubble. "This is the first time I can remember him willingly engaging in subterfuge for his own benefit. Except for that time he pretended to be me in order to get you in the closet the night of our graduation. But I don't know if that technically counts."

"You knew about that?" Arlie suddenly felt like someone had dialed the office thermostat up by about twenty degrees.

"Please," Mason said. "You don't think every pathetic preppie piece of shit in the school came up afterward to congratulate me for scoring seven minutes with Arlie Banks?"

She hadn't exactly imagined that scenario.

"Of course," he continued, "when you didn't say a word about it to me, I suspected that you knew, too."

"You suspected correctly," she confirmed.

"The thing I find interesting," Mason said, turning to face them, "is that both events have something in common. You."

"I'm not sure what I'm supposed to do with that information," Arlie said.

Strolling back toward the desk, Mason seated himself on the corner. "I probably seem like the least likely person to defend Samuel's actions from the present vantage, but I would point out that having a father like ours can incline one to—" he paused, as if looking for the right words "—less than optimal behaviors."

Arlie sensed the unspoken depths in that statement.

"Will you do me a favor?" Mason asked.

"What's that?"

"Take a week and think about it." He rose from the desk to stand next to her. "We can hold your resignation until you've had more time."

"I appreciate you being willing to do that," Arlie said. "But after everything that's happened, I really think it's best that I go."

Mason nodded, looking uncharacteristically melancholy. "I understand."

"Well." Arlie retrieved her notebook and added it to the box before hefting it onto her hip. "I think that's it."

Kassidy picked up her Burberry trench coat and followed her toward the door. "Good seeing you, Kane."

"Likewise, Kassidy *the brain* Nichols."

"For future reference, I would vastly prefer you not call me that."

Arlie liked to think she knew her best friend's face

at least half as well as Kassidy knew hers, and what she read there was not exactly displeasure at Mason.

"I look forward to the future occasion where I might prove my ability to honor that request."

They turned to go.

"Arlie?" Mason called when they had almost reached the door.

She looked back at him. "Yes?"

Familiar mischief banished the gloom from his features. "How did you know?"

"How did I know what?" she asked.

"The closet. How did you know it wasn't me?"

His question spun her backward in their shared past. A flickering montage of her life's significant moments spooled by her mind's eye until she arrived at the night in question. Through the vantage of her eighteen-year-old self, she watched Mason exiting through the back-door only to reappear minutes later at the mouth of the hallway.

One of Mason's regular posse had come up to him then, clapping him on the shoulder before pressing a red plastic cup of foamy beer into his hand. Which is when he had lifted his left hand and with the tip of his index finger, attempted to push a pair of nonexistent glasses up his nose.

She must have witnessed this precise gesture at least a thousand times.

Mason—the real Mason—had gotten contacts on his thirteenth birthday. Arlie remembered because he had beckoned her over to look at them, insisting she lean in close enough to see if she could detect their ethereal edges.

Of course, he had tried to kiss her when she was close enough.

The present Mason hung there, awaiting her answer.

"Research," she said, sending him an enigmatic smile.

# Seventeen

Samuel had often felt it was his father's back, not face, he would be able to pick out of a crowd.

Parker Kane's lectures always began this way. With his father staring out of some window, hands clasped behind his suit jacket, silence radiating from him like an arctic wind as he gazed contemplatively into the middle distance.

When he was a boy, Samuel had assumed it was because his father was so disappointed in whatever it was he had done or failed to do that he needed time to search for the words to describe it.

Now he recognized it for exactly what it was.

A tactic to further unnerve him.

He had been summoned to his father's office by a text from Charlotte at 6:00 a.m.

*Your father would like to see you this morning.*

Samuel had known it was coming, but it didn't stop his stomach from knotting all the same. When he'd arrived at his father's office at precisely eight o'clock, Charlotte had looked at him with the kind of pitying, hangdog expression usually reserved for people being marched to the gallows.

One look at his father's desk confirmed that was his fate.

Next to a large manila envelope was what appeared to be a print copy of an article on the *PhillyGossip* website.

*"Sex, Lies, and Candy! Not-so-Sweet Scandal at Kane Foods," the title screamed.*

He quickly scanned it, his eyes snagging on a series of words that painted the whole, lurid picture. "A source close to the Kanes" had not only confirmed Arlie's recent involvement in a "devastating corporate espionage case," but hinted that her romantic involvement with the CEO of Kane Foods International may not be "purely romantic" in nature. An unstated, but heavily implied, suggestion that Samuel, and Kane Foods by extension, was guilty of shady business practices.

He had no doubt that the "source" was Taegan but given this context, realized Arlie had never been the true target.

"I've often wondered," his father said, not bothering to face him, "exactly what kind of pleasure you derive from humiliating me."

Samuel's jaw clenched, his teeth grinding together. There was no correct answer to this question. It wasn't even a question, really. It was an accusation. A verdict.

One Samuel had let stand in so many of these conversations.

"None whatsoever." Samuel dropped into one of the chairs reserved for inferiors who were required to address him across the moat of his desk. "But then, I don't consider a sensationalized story on a gossip website cause for humiliation."

"Henry had mentioned that you'd been rather...*distracted* on the yacht. It seems he's having some misgivings about continuing with his investment," his father continued. "Of course, at the time, I reassured him that you are fully committed to our partnership.

"Which makes me look even more foolish. That I wouldn't know that my own son was consorting with a woman accused of corporate espionage." His father tapped the pads of his thumbs together, still addressing his remarks to the Philadelphia skyline. The morning sun had crept high enough on the horizon to film the skyscraper windows with molten gold. "At least she had the decency to resign."

A leaden weight gathered in Samuel's stomach. Losing the confidence of an investor was one thing.

Losing Arlie Banks was another entirely.

But then, he hadn't lost her.

He had never had her to begin with.

She had failed to answer any of his texts, or return any of his many calls. Not that he knew what he would say if she had. And in the end, when it came to Arlie, he had never known what to say.

"Of course, I've reached out to our media contacts about distancing Kane Foods from her."

Samuel's hands tightened on the wooden arms of the chair. "Whatever you decide where I'm concerned, you will leave Arlie Banks out of it."

At last, his father turned to him. "Do you honestly think you're in any kind of position to make those kinds of demands?"

"I think I'm in the perfect position to do so." He met his father's icy glare. "You forget that I've been on the back end of every deal that Kane Foods has negotiated. I know every secret, every cut corner, every oiled palm. However unpleasant you find your current circumstances, I can promise that if *I* decide to talk to the gossip rags, or any media outlet, for that matter, the Kane family name will be on the lips of those leeches for years to come."

His father's tight, parsimonious smile melted into corrosive sneer. "I suppose it shouldn't surprise me that you would so easily turn your back on your family. After all, when Arlie's mother stole—"

"No!" Samuel's fist came down hard enough on the desk to make his father's pen jump. He had no memory of standing, no consciousness of anything other than the blood thundering in his ears. "Your pathetic acolytes may have accepted your accusation without question, but Mom told me the *real* reason you got rid of Margaret Banks."

His father's face looked like a punctured balloon.

"Mom was going to leave you." Speaking these words out loud filled him with savage satisfaction. "She was going to leave you, and Margaret was going to help. And you know what? I wish she had. At least then she would have had a few precious months of freedom before she died."

Despite his best efforts, Samuel's voice grew harsh with emotion at these last words.

Eight days.

Eight days had transpired between the time Arlie's mother had been fired and his mother learning she had stage three breast cancer. Whatever plans she'd had for an escape had taken a rapid back seat to the endless parade of doctors and specialists who'd made their way to Fair Weather Hall.

His father's laugh was as thin and dry as rice paper. "With all those books you read, it's no wonder you imagine your life to be a gothic tragedy."

Samuel ignored the comment. "You ruined an innocent woman, but you will *not* do the same to her daughter."

"But is she innocent?" His father lazily brushed the paper on his desk, a gesture deliberately designed to let Samuel know just how unmoved he'd been by his display of temper. "It seems she's managed to make a good deal of trouble for herself. And many others."

"You have no idea what really happened."

"And no desire to learn. Still." His father paced around the end of his desk, pausing before a bronze bust of Plato. "If this is where we're *planting our flag*, then I suppose what I have to propose might be of value to you."

"Go on," Samuel said, his tongue tasting of metal and bile.

"I will make sure that our press agents communicate that we have nothing but positive feelings for Miss Banks and that she departs with our full support. If—" his father paused, clearly relishing his next words "—you are willing to release a public statement that you are not, nor ever were, romantically involved with her."

"I won't do that," Samuel said without hesitation.

"You would deny Miss Banks the opportunity to have that kind of support after her recent difficulties?"

Leave it to his father to make an act of basic human decency seem like a generous gift.

"At the price of my having to lie about her place in my life?" Samuel challenged. "Absolutely."

"And what place would that be, exactly?" his father asked.

"That's up to Arlie," Samuel said. "All I know is that I won't agree to any arrangement where her exclusion is required."

A look of shrewd amusement sharpened his father's features.

"Tell me," he said, dropping a hand on the back of his desk chair. "*If* I were to offer you the chance to step down as the CEO of Kane Foods in exchange for Kane Foods' public media support of Miss Banks, would you accept?"

Weeks ago, the answer to this question might have required hours, maybe even days of thought. For years he had worked, pouring his time, his energy, his *soul* into his father's empire. Only to realize that it had never been the title, or the salary, or even the industry prestige he wanted.

He had wanted the legacy.

His *father's* legacy.

To be Parker Kane's heir in the truest sense.

Seen. Acknowledged. Accepted.

Now, he allowed himself to grieve for the loss of that dream.

"I might. *If*," Samuel said, mimicking his father's pronunciation, "I'm allowed an additional condition."

"Which is?"

Samuel took a step forward to stand directly opposite the man whose shadow had fallen across every aspect of his life. "I want you to look me in the eye and tell me why you resent me so much."

The Kane patriarch's gaze narrowed, his cheeks going gray, his lips a bloodless white.

A cheerful succession of raps echoed from the office door, which swung open before he granted permission to enter.

To Samuel's complete and utter shock, Mason stepped in, a smile on his lips and a coffee cup in his hand.

"Sorry I'm late. That traffic." Mason slurped from the black plastic lid and shook his head. "Catch me up."

A hot filament of dread sizzled in Samuel's gut. He hadn't seen his brother since he'd revealed the details of his plan to Arlie. But he was almost certain that Mason knew by now exactly what he'd tried to do.

Was that why he had come? To gloat over Samuel's rapid demise?

The tension on their father's bearing eased as it so often did when Mason arrived on the scene. "Your presence wasn't requested at this meeting, Mason. What we're discussing doesn't concern you."

"Oh, I beg to differ." Mason slid into the chair beside the one Samuel had vacated. "Seeing as my brother hired Arlie Banks as part of an effort to eject me from the coveted spot of CMO, it concerns me *deeply*."

*Shit*.

Their father was silent for a moment, clearly attempting to decide if arguing with Mason was worth the battle.

It never was.

Aware that he was still standing, Samuel resumed his seat, a symbolic acceptance of his presence and admission of guilt. Their father followed suit, pulling out his wide wing-backed leather chair and settling himself into it.

Parker Kane cleared his throat. Something. Important. Would. Now. Be. Said.

"My whole life, I've worked to make the Kane name synonymous with quality and integrity. And when something threatens the legacy I've attempted to build, I deal with it expediently, regardless of the source. Samuel has refused my offer to mitigate the damage he has caused while retaining his position, and for that reason, I feel that it is best that Samuel step down as CEO."

Mason leaned forward in his chair, his head cocked at a curious angle. "And what would Samuel receive in exchange for his willing exit?"

Pleasure at Mason's interest in his plans was heaped on their father's face like caviar on a toast point. "Miss Banks will receive our full recommendation and support in any future endeavor."

"Huh." Mason nodded slowly. "Yeah, that's a no for me."

"You don't think we should offer Miss Banks a recommendation?" their father asked, silvery eyebrows raised.

Acid ate at Samuel's stomach. *We.* As always, that *we* included Mason and his father alone.

"No," Mason said. "I don't think Samuel should step down as CEO."

Samuel couldn't tell who was more surprised, himself or their father.

"I beg your pardon?" Parker said.

"I don't think Samuel should step down as CEO." Mason set his coffee cup down on their father's desk with a decisive thump.

"Perhaps you would be kind enough to share your reasoning behind this."

In that moment, Samuel felt himself hoping the reasons would be purely selfish in nature. Transition in CEOs could send a red flag up to potential investors. It would be better to force Samuel to stay on during the resulting fallout for his own humiliation.

"Because Samuel is the reason Kane Foods has sustained a 10% revenue growth rate year over year since he was appointed CEO and deep down, you know dismissing him would be cataclysmically stupid."

Had Mason walked into the room, hauled back, and clocked him in the jaw, Samuel would have accepted this as his due. He'd rolled the dice and lost. Fair was fair.

But this?

This left him more stunned than any knockout punch ever could.

His twin going to bat for him in front of the father whose favor he clearly owned? After Samuel had done his level best to sabotage him?

"Your brother hired a woman for the express purpose of attempting to lure you into an affair that would result in your dismissal. You don't think that's grounds for his resignation?"

"First of all," Mason said, "she's not just *a woman*. She's Arlie Banks, and she's a wonderfully talented food stylist. I would have hired her in a hot minute, with or without my brother's *scheming*."

An exceedingly unwelcome flush of heat erupted beneath Samuel's collar when Mason pinned him with a pointed look.

"Second, I've personally broken that rule on at least six very memorable occasions. The only difference is that Samuel is too pathetically honest not to get caught."

"Romances within the workplace compromise productivity. They can lead to potential legal consequences—" their father sputtered.

"Did you or did you not meet our mother working at the soda fountain at the Sunset Drive-in in Conshohocken?" Mason asked.

"Mom never told me that!" Samuel objected.

"She knew it would offend your orderly soul," Mason replied.

"That was the circumstance of our original acquaintance," Parker admitted.

Though he couldn't be certain, Samuel would have sworn he saw a subtle sheen coating their father's eyes.

"Look," Mason said. "Every one of us in this room knows that you have the resources to shape this narrative however you want. My personal recommendation is to come down on *PhillyGossip* like a ton of bricks. And when you find the source of this article, make them pay, and pay again. Make them rue the day they ever typed the name Kane."

Samuel felt a slick of pleasure at the idea. At Taegan subject to the same scrutiny she'd brought to Arlie.

Their father stood, wandering back to his spot at the window.

"And if I should decide Samuel's resignation remains the best course of action?"

"Then you'll have mine to go with it," Mason said. "Marlowe's too, if you're curious."

Samuel glanced at his twin, not fully sure what he expected to see, his mind buzzing with the one question.

*Why would you do this for me after what I tried to do to you?*

Mason grinned. The one answer he could and would always give clear in his eyes.

*Because I can.*

On an exhale that could have moved a mountain range, their father faced them. "I suppose, in this particular instance, maintaining our current structure might be the wisest course of action."

"That current structure *will* include Arlie Banks," Samuel said. "Whether or not she'll have me after all that's happened."

Their father stiffened. "I can't think of any reason why I should accept such a stipulation."

"Because it lends credibility to our position about the article," Mason pointed out. "The fact that you insisted on keeping her with the company despite the rumors is practically a recommendation in and of itself."

Crafty. Appealing to their father's ego.

But then, Mason had always been more effective when it came to navigating the waters of flattery.

Heaving a beleaguered sigh, Parker Kane shook his head.

"Fine. But should there be negative consequences to any part of this arrangement, I will hold you both personally responsible."

There had been times when Samuel had refused to

speak and times when words failed him. But never in his memory had there been a moment so pure and rare that words felt like a betrayal.

A victory had been won.

The polite tap on their father's office door interrupted the tense silence.

"What?" he barked.

The door inched open, revealing Charlotte's concerned visage. "Sorry to interrupt," she said. "You have a call with Vibrant Health in five minutes."

"I believe we're finished here." He looked from Samuel to Mason.

"Totally finished on this end," Mason said. "Samuel?"

"Completely."

Together, they exited their father's office. Samuel's knees were rubbery, sweat drying on his clammy skin. Walking down the hallway toward the elevator, the brothers fell into step. Legs of precisely the same length finding the same stride. Twins after all.

They stood side by side, waiting for the car to come.

"I'm not sure why you did that," Samuel said, "but I want you to know that I'm grateful. After what I tried to do—"

"What you tried to do," Mason said, "was get me booted from a role I've clearly resented for years by reuniting me with a woman you mistakenly believed I loved. You absolute bastard. How dare you?"

"Point taken."

Mason nodded to a pair of admins who ducked their heads and giggled the second they passed. "*I'm* the one who should apologize."

A sentence Samuel had never in his life expected to hear. "For what?"

"For letting you shoulder the lion's share of responsibility as long as you have." His brother glanced toward the expanse of windows at the end of the hall. "I guess I had always assumed that you took on as much as you did because you wanted to. Not because I was such a fuck-up that you had to."

"You're not a fuck-up." Samuel smirked. "Just especially gifted at evading responsibility."

"Accurate," Mason agreed. "I just never really wanted this, you know? The whole corporate-owned soul thing."

"It's not like any of us were given much choice," Samuel said. And this was true. From the time they'd been old enough to lurch down their family home's marbled halls, they'd been guided through a carefully orchestrated regime of activities designed to prepare them for the life their father had in mind. They had arrived at an entirely different territory now.

"So what are you going to do?" his brother asked.

"About what?"

Mason raised an eyebrow at him. "About the fact that you're madly in love with Arlie Banks?"

The denial rose in Samuel's throat, but he no longer had the strength to pretend.

He *was* in love with her.

He had been in love with her.

"She has no reason to forgive me," he said.

"I did," Mason said. "Don't you think there's even the slightest chance that she might understand how what you did had everything to do with our father and nothing to do with her?"

Samuel just stared at his brother, shocked by this unexpected insight.

"Maybe you could try to look a *little* less surprised that I'm capable of empathetic thought?" Mason asked.

"I'm sorry," Samuel said. "I just don't know how she could want to be with me after all that's happened."

The elevator dinged, burnished-metal doors sliding open.

They stepped in.

Mason stepped toward him, dropping his hands on Samuel's shoulders.

"You are Samuel Kane. You graduated magna cum laude. You have pulled off seventeen mergers deemed impossible by *Forbes*. Beyond which, I happen to know that you're remarkably good looking. Go. Get. The. Girl."

# Eighteen

"Arlington Banks."

Kassidy's voice sounded disembodied. Surreal. Muffled by several layers of Arlie's blanket cocoon, which also kept the terrible daylight out. The world beneath these supremely comforting fuzzy layers was quiet and manageable. Soft. Dim.

"Arlington Quartermaine Banks," Kassidy repeated.

"Yes?" Arlie said, not moving.

"We are not having this conversation through a Pottery Barn throw blanket."

The voice was closer now.

Arlie was getting good at identifying the direction and distance of the various sounds in her new kingdom without the benefit of sight.

Garbage trucks.

Ambulances.

The TV.

The refrigerator's compressor.

Begrudgingly, she lifted the edge of her blanket just enough to squint one eye at her best friend, who knelt next to the couch that had become Arlie's home, restaurant and entertainment center over the last week.

"I love you," Kassidy said, reaching a hand beneath the blanket to find Arlie's. "But this has got to stop."

"What's that?" Wrapping an arm around her knees, Arlie drew them tighter into her chest. This had become her default setting. Comfort achieved only when she condensed the swirling chaos of her life into the smallest possible configuration.

"It's been a week, and you haven't moved from that position."

"What's the point?" Indeed, this had been the mantra that seemed to swim through her head any time she contemplated an action that would draw her out of her misery.

"The point is, a couple more days and your ass is going to fuse with my couch. This was not at all the roommate scenario I had in mind when I invited you to stay with me."

"Sorry to disappoint—"

Cruelly and without warning, her blanket was whipped away, leaving her exposed and blinking like a vampire in the sun. "Hey!" she protested.

"That's it." Kassidy balled up the blanket and shot it across the room. "You will peel yourself out of those crusty pajamas. You will marinate in a hot shower. You will put actual adult clothing on your body and you will come with me to the Blue Note, where I will procure a stud to make out with you."

Arlie picked at a crusty spot on the knee of her pajama bottoms that might have been ice cream or gravy. She wasn't sure which. "I'm really not in a making-out mood."

The truth was, Arlie now lived in mortal terror that no kiss would ever live up to Samuel Kane's. In college, all kisses had been measured against their furtive exchange in the closet. Now she had much *much* more to reference. The chances that any random bar hookup would bring her anything but disappointment were very slim.

"Well, I am," Kassidy said. "And seeing as you're not required to pay rent, this is the price of your room and board. That we go out and find men."

Rolling her tired, stinging eyes up to her best friend, Arlie calculated the odds that she could wiggle her way out of this.

The odds weren't good.

Drawing in a deep breath, she sat up and obeyed Kassidy's command.

Showered, shaved and squeaky clean, Arlie emerged to find her best friend on the other side of the door with a silky bathrobe and her makeup bag. "Surprise!"

"And what, I ask you, is the meaning of this?"

"Indulge your exceedingly patient best friend in a night of nostalgia." Kassidy pushed a damp lock of hair away from Arlie's forehead. "You always let me do your makeup when we went out together."

"When I was fifteen and my mother wouldn't let me wear lipstick."

*"Please."* Kassidy's eyes were wide in supplication, her palms pressed together in front of her chic Prada top.

"Okay." Shrugging into the bathrobe and dropping her towel, Arlie allowed herself to be led to Kassidy's room, where, a mere thirty minutes later, she blinked at her completely transformed reflection in the vanity mirror.

"I don't want to brag or anything," Kassidy said, stepping back to admire her handiwork, "but holy shit."

Arlie was inclined to agree.

She'd avoided meeting her own eye in the months since she'd been fired from *Gastronomie*, aside from quick checks to confirm she didn't have lipstick on her teeth or mascara on her cheek.

Now, she looked at herself.

*Really* looked.

She was still there.

Still her.

Kassidy's doorbell rang, echoing through the condo.

"I think it's for you." An alarmingly knowing look brightened her friend's eyes.

Arlie laughed, leaning into the mirror to thumb one of her dramatically sweeping lashes. "No one knows I'm here."

When Kassidy didn't respond, Arlie's heart began to gallop. "Do they?" she asked, fully aware of the edge of desperation in her voice.

"I guess you'll have to see." An enigmatic smile shaped Kassidy's lips.

"Why do you do these things to me?" Arlie asked, pushing past her into the hallway.

"Because I love you, that's why," Kassidy called after her.

Gathering the silky robe tighter around her, Arlie

padded barefoot to the foyer. Disengaging the dead bolt, she swung the door wide.

And there, to her complete and absolute astonishment, was Samuel Kane.

In a tuxedo.

Caught in some strange interval between fantasy and reality, Arlie had a flash of how this moment would unfold in one of the soap operas her mother had so religiously followed. Dramatic lighting. Tight camera angle. Golden hair tumbling over her shoulder. Erratic breath pushing her breasts outward, hand pressed to her sternum, glossy lips forming the breathy sentence, "What are you doing here?"

What came out of her mouth instead was "Whaaa?"

Samuel's mouth opened. Closed. Opened again. Clearly, this had not been the greeting he'd been expecting. And Arlie suspected that the speech he had prepared for this occasion went out the window.

"I have something for you," he finally said.

As the initial shock of his presence wore off, additional details began to surface in Arlie's vision. The arm still bound in the sling rested against his chest, a leather padfolio tucked beneath it. He liberated it with his free hand and slid it into hers.

The leather was satiny in her fingers. Warm from his body heat. "Roses are considered a more traditional apology offering, you know."

"I was hoping you might appreciate a more practical gift," he said. "May I come in?"

She was on the point of telling him that it wasn't her house, and therefore he'd require the permission of its owner, when she noticed that Kassidy had made herself conspicuously absent.

Arlie stepped to the side.

"Nice place," Samuel said.

"Not mine." Moving past him, Arlie plopped down on the couch, the padfolio in her lap. "Make yourself at home."

Samuel hung in the entryway, green eyes skating from the couch, to the love seat, to the club chair opposite them, clearly trying to calculate where he should go.

The man had been inside of her and yet couldn't quite navigate how to share a couch.

Feeling a tug of protective tenderness at his plight, Arlie patted the cushion next to hers. He crossed the room and sat, not quite next to her but not exactly at the other end of the couch.

Progress.

"I'm assuming you'd like me to open this now?" Arlie asked.

"Only if you'd like to put me out of my misery."

Truth be told, Arlie wasn't sure that she did. In the dim world of her blanket cocoon, she could stoke the coals of her anger, the humiliation she had endured. But now, with Samuel seated near her, the main thing his presence did was remind her how much she liked being in it.

The bastard.

Sliding her fingers along the folder's crease, she opened it. Documents had been tucked in the pockets on either side. Her stomach flipped as she ran headlong into *Gastronomie's* logo.

"Read it," Samuel urged, clearly seeing the blind panic on her face.

Scanning down through the address block and

lengthy formal greeting, her eye snagged on a particular word.

*Apologies.*

Running back to the beginning of the line, she read it in full.

> *We have received additional information from Mr. Samuel Kane's counsel regarding the events surrounding your departure and are prepared to return the settlement collected as a result of your civil matter. Please contact our offices at your earliest convenience so we may discuss the necessary arrangements.*

The words began to blur as the sheets of paper trembled in Arlie's hands. Her knuckles were white. Heart throbbing in her chest.

Could it actually be?

"How?" was the only question she could manage.

"I gave a copy of Taegan's *PhillyGossip* smear job and the information about Project Impact she'd been attempting to blackmail you into giving her to our lawyers. They then contacted *Gastronomie* to make the management team aware of this situation, and suggested that we might negotiate an arrangement instead of making this an extensive and embarrassing legal matter. Kane Foods is notoriously protective of its employees, after all."

Arlie blinked at him. "But I'm not an employee of Kane Foods any longer."

Samuel cut his eyes toward the other document in the folder.

With fingers still twitching, Arlie pulled it from the

sheath. An offer letter inviting her to rejoin Kane Foods International at a significant raise.

Looking up from the paper, Arlie examined Samuel's face. What she saw was a tangle of many things. Pride. Terror. Remorse. Hope.

"Why?" she asked.

"I don't know if you can forgive me," he said. "But I need you to know that I'm sorry. I'm sorry that I wasn't man enough to tell you how I felt when we were teenagers. I'm sorry I pretended to be my brother so I could kiss you. I'm sorry that I hired you thinking that you might still want him." His broad, suit-clad shoulders sank, his gaze fixed on her. "Most of all, I'm sorry that the morning after we were together the first time, I didn't tell you that there isn't a single thing that you could say or do that would change the way I feel about you."

Tears stung Arlie's eyes.

Now it was her turn to be speechless.

Leaning in closer, Samuel gently thumbed a tear from her cheek.

"I came here to ask you something I should have asked you a long time ago."

"What's that?" Arlie sniffed.

Shifting on the sofa, he turned to her, taking her hand in his. "Arlington Banks. Will you go to the prom with me?"

"Prom?" One great hiccup of laughter bubbled out of her through her streaming tears. "What prom?"

"The prom that's happening tonight at the Lennox Finch Preparatory events hall," he said.

"But I don't have a dress," she protested.

Behind her, Kassidy gave an excessively exaggerated *ahem*.

Arlie turned and saw her best friend holding a garment bag aloft. "Would you look at that? I just happen to have a prom dress right here."

"You *knew*!" Arlie accused, elated as she was incredulous.

"How the hell do you think he knew where you were staying?" Kassidy sauntered across the room and laid the garment bag gently over the club chair. "This young man not only asked for my assistance, he asked for my permission. Which, benevolent creature that I am, I graciously gave him."

"After she told me that she'd rip my spine out through my ass if I hurt you," Samuel added.

"That part is exceedingly important." Kassidy pointed a finger at him, the effect greatly compromised by her unabashed grin.

Before that moment, Arlie had never felt happiness so large, so expansive, that it registered as an actual pain in her chest. Having the greatest worry of her life completely taken away. Glancing back and forth between her best friend and the boy she had adored, hearing them joke with one another. Could this actually be real?

Could this really be her life?

"Well?" Kassidy prodded Arlie's shoulder. "Are you going to answer the man or sit there ruining the makeup I so skillfully applied?"

Dabbing the corners of her eyes with her borrowed bathrobe, Arlie nodded. "Yes," she said. "Yes, Samuel Kane, I'll go to the prom with you."

Samuel smiled like a man who hadn't known what

a smile was until that precise second. Using his uninjured arm to steady himself, he leaned in and kissed her.

She could taste the salt of tears on her own lips as
they met his. Forgiveness asked and freely given. Years
and hurts and missed chances mended by the feeling of
his mouth on hers.

"All right, you two," Kassidy scolded, shoving the
dress at Arlie. "That's enough of that. Let's get you
dressed and on your way, madam."

They retreated to Kassidy's room, where she zipped
Arlie into a vintage floor-length Versace of the deepest
blue, a slit in the rustling silk rising high up her thigh.

Had she lived another hundred years, Arlie knew she
would never forget the way Samuel looked at her when
she emerged. A mix of hunger and wonder and pride
that lit a fire somewhere in her soul.

"Shall we?" he said, offering her his good arm.

"Don't do anything I wouldn't do." Kassidy called
after them as they descended the stairs together.

"That rules out, like, one and a half things," Arlie
called back.

Her best friend's laugh danced like bells on the air
until it was broken off by the door closing.

A glossy black vintage Packard limousine waited
for them at the curb, the driver standing ready to open
their door.

Samuel handed Arlie in, carefully ducking in after
her.

Once they were both inside, the air around them
crackled with barely restrained electricity.

What was it about limos anyway?

In that thick silence, Samuel traced her bare skin

through the slit in her skirt, beginning at her knee and wandering lazily up her thigh.

"That's a good way to get yourself in trouble," Arlie breathed.

"Think you can wait until we get to Lennox Finch?" Samuel's finger dipped beneath the silk, sliding over her sex through the lace of her panties. "I may or may not have a very specific fantasy I'd like to enlist your cooperation in."

"I can if you can." Summoning every ounce of will-power she possessed, Arlie picked up Samuel's hand and put it back in his own lap.

Which was a *very* big mistake. He was already hard.

"Are you absolutely sure you don't want me to take care of this for you?" Arlie ran her hand along his length. "We can't have you walking into the prom with a trouser tent."

With a groan of frustration, Samuel mirrored her gesture, removing her hand from his lap. "Give me a minute to think about profit and loss statements."

"And here I thought those would be just as likely to get you hard."

His lips twisted in a wry smile. "You're not entirely wrong about that."

After a journey that seemed to last five minutes and forever, the limo pulled up in front of the prep school's sprawling edifice. A place that transported her back through many years to a much younger and braver self.

They strolled arm-in-arm down the long colonnade that Arlie had always felt belonged in a monastery more than a school.

Music pulsed out to them on the night air in a whoosh

as the double doors to the gym opened and they made their way in.

Arlie froze in the entryway, her mouth dropping open.

A hand-painted banner bearing the words *I Left My Heart in San Francisco* was hung just beyond the door. But it wasn't just any painted sign.

It looked *exactly* like the one she remembered laboring over only hours before the original prom was set to start.

"How did you—" she began, but the words died away as she saw the rest.

The San Francisco skyline sprawling along the eastern wall. An arch of silver and red balloons before a black-velvet drop cloth.

Save for a few very minor details—such as a full bar—it was an exact replica of the prom they hadn't attended together.

"I had to recreate it from what I could find in old yearbook photos," Samuel said, leading her toward the dance floor.

As they approached, she began to recognize some of the faces among the gown and tuxedo-clad crowd already populating the gymnasium.

Mason, very James Bond in all black, gave her a thumbs-up behind the back of a woman who could have fallen straight off fashion runway.

Charlotte, conspicuously pretending not to watch Mason and his date as she leaned in to say something to the bar attendant.

Marlowe and her fiancé, Neil, who lingered near the bar's other end.

An assortment of other friends and colleagues that

she suspected Kassidy would be joining at some point in the evening.

Samuel paused when they were directly under the disco ball scattering fractured lights over the walls and wood floor of the basketball court.

"Dance?" he asked.

"First dance?" she teased. "Or last dance."

Samuel stepped closer, drawing her into him with his hand on her lower back. Mindful of the sling, she melted into him. Arms around his waist. Cheek against his chest. His chin resting atop her head like an anchor. A single point that solidified her place in the world.

"No dance will ever be our last dance, Arlie Banks," he said.

With the galaxy of lights moving over and around them and the secret music of his heartbeat in her ear, Arlie knew it was true.

\* \* \* \* \*

*If you loved Arlie and Samuel,*
*don't miss Mason Kane's story,*
*the next book in The Kane Heirs series*
*by Cynthia St. Aubin.*

*Available August 2022 from Harlequin Desire.*

**HQN**

*Welcome to Four Corners Ranch, Maisey Yates's newest miniseries, where the West is still wild...and when a cowboy needs a wife, he decides to find her the old-fashioned way!*

*Evelyn Moore can't believe she's agreed to uproot her city life to become Oregon cowboy and single dad Sawyer Garrett's mail-order bride. Her love for his tiny daughter is instant. Her feelings for Sawyer are...more complicated. Her gruff cowboy husband ignites a thrilling desire in her, but Sawyer is determined to keep their marriage all about the baby. But what happens if Evelyn wants it all?*

The front door opened, and a man came out. He had on a black cowboy hat, and he was holding a baby. Those were the first two details she took in, but then there was... Well, there was the whole rest of him.

Evelyn could feel his eyes on her from some fifty feet away, could see the piercing blue color. His nose was straight and strong, as was his jaw. His lips were remarkable, and she didn't think she had ever really found lips on a man all that remarkable. He had the sort of symmetrical good looks that might make a man almost too pretty, but he was saved from that by a scar that edged through the corner of his mouth, creating a thick white line that disrupted the symmetry there. He was tall. Well over six feet, and broad.

And his arms were...

Good Lord.

He was wearing a short-sleeved black T-shirt, and he cradled the tiny baby in the crook of a massive bicep and forearm. He could easily lift bales of hay and throw them around. Hell, he could probably easily lift the truck and throw it around.

He was beautiful. Objectively, absolutely beautiful.

But there was something more than that. Because as he walked toward her, she felt like he was stealing increments of her breath, emptying her lungs. She'd seen handsome men before. She'd been around celebrities who were touted as the sexiest men on the planet.

But she had never felt anything quite like this.

Because this wasn't just about how he looked on the outside, though it was sheer masculine perfection; it was about what he did to her insides. Like he had taken the blood in her veins and replaced it with fire. And she could say with absolute honesty she had never once in all of her days wanted to grab a stranger and fling herself at him, and push them both into the nearest closet, bedroom, whatever, and…

Well, everything.

But she felt it, right then and there with him.

And there was something about the banked heat in his blue eyes that made her think he might feel exactly the same way.

And suddenly she was terrified of all the freedom. Giddy with it, which went right along with that joy/terror paradox from before.

She didn't know anyone here. She had come without anyone's permission or approval. She was just here. With this man. And there was nothing to stop them from…anything.

Except he was holding a baby and his sister was standing right to her left. But otherwise…

She really hoped that he was Sawyer. Because if he was Wolf, it was going to be awkward.

"Evelyn," he said. And goose bumps broke out over her arms. And she knew. Because he was the same man who had told her that she would be making him meat loaf whether she liked it or not.

And suddenly the reason it had felt distinctly sexual this time became clear.

"Yes," she responded.

"Sawyer," he said. "Sawyer Garrett." And then he absurdly took a step forward and held his hand out. To shake. And she was going to have to… touch him. Touch him and not melt into a puddle at his feet.

*Find out what happens next in Evelyn and Sawyer's marriage deal in* Unbridled Cowboy, *the unmissable first installment in Maisey Yates's new Four Corners Ranch miniseries.*

*Don't miss* Unbridled Cowboy *by New York Times bestselling author Maisey Yates, available May 2022 wherever HQN books and ebooks are sold.*

HQNBooks.com

# Get 4 FREE REWARDS!

**We'll send you 2 FREE Books plus 2 FREE Mystery Gifts.**

**FREE**
Value Over
**$20**

Both the **Harlequin® Desire** and **Harlequin Presents®** series feature compelling novels filled with passion, sensuality and intriguing scandals.

---

**YES!** Please send me 2 FREE novels from the Harlequin Desire or Harlequin Presents series and my 2 FREE gifts (gifts are worth about $10 retail). After receiving them, if I don't wish to receive any more books, I can return the shipping statement marked "cancel." If I don't cancel, I will receive 6 brand-new Harlequin Presents Larger-Print books every month and be billed just $5.80 each in the U.S. or $5.99 each in Canada, a savings of at least 11% off the cover price or 6 Harlequin Desire books every month and be billed just $4.55 each in the U.S. or $5.24 each in Canada, a savings of at least 13% off the cover price. It's quite a bargain! Shipping and handling is just 50¢ per book in the U.S. and $1.25 per book in Canada.* I understand that accepting the 2 free books and gifts places me under no obligation to buy anything. I can always return a shipment and cancel at any time. The free books and gifts are mine to keep no matter what I decide.

Choose one: ☐ **Harlequin Desire**     ☐ **Harlequin Presents Larger-Print**
                (225/326 HDN GNND)             (176/376 HDN GNWY)

Name (please print)

Address                                                        Apt. #

City                         State/Province                     Zip/Postal Code

**Email:** Please check this box ☐ if you would like to receive newsletters and promotional emails from Harlequin Enterprises ULC and its affiliates. You can unsubscribe anytime.

---

Mail to the **Harlequin Reader Service:**
**IN U.S.A.:** P.O. Box 1341, Buffalo, NY 14240-8531
**IN CANADA:** P.O. Box 603, Fort Erie, Ontario L2A 5X3

**Want to try 2 free books from another series!** Call 1-800-873-8635 or visit www.ReaderService.com.

---

*Terms and prices subject to change without notice. Prices do not include sales taxes, which will be charged (if applicable) based on your state or country of residence. Canadian residents will be charged applicable taxes. Offer not valid in Quebec. This offer is limited to one order per household. Books received may not be as shown. Not valid for current subscribers to the Harlequin Presents or Harlequin Desire series. All orders subject to approval. Credit or debit balances in a customer's account(s) may be offset by any other outstanding balance owed by or to the customer. Please allow 4 to 6 weeks for delivery. Offer available while quantities last.

**Your Privacy**—Your information is being collected by Harlequin Enterprises ULC, operating as Harlequin Reader Service. For a complete summary of the information we collect, how we use this information and to whom it is disclosed, please visit our privacy notice located at corporate.harlequin.com/privacy-notice. From time to time we may also exchange your personal information with reputable third parties. If you wish to opt out of this sharing of your personal information, please visit readerservice.com/consumerschoice or call 1-800-873-8635. **Notice to California Residents**—Under California law, you have specific rights to control and access your data. For more information on these rights and how to exercise them, visit corporate.harlequin.com/california-privacy.

HDHP22